ACCLA

MW01135598

"This award recognize
genres. Your book has recei
a 5 Cup Rating."
—Review by Matilda, for Coffee Time Romance & More
On A JOYFUL BREAK

*"Ms. Craver penned this story with such emotion that it was easy for me
to feel as if the story was unfolding before me firsthand."*
—Review by Diana Coyle for Night Owl Romance Reviews
Top Pick, 5 stars on A JOYFUL BREAK

*"A JOYFUL BREAK is a light, sweet story that will warm your heart
and leave you with the feeling that all is right in the world."*
— award-winning author Karen Wiesner
5 stars, Book One in Dreams of Plain Daughters Series

*"JUDITH'S PLACE provides readers with an inside look at the
Amish community that is more in depth than other Amish books that I've
read. . .It wasn't a sappy story, the tension and anxiety was real. A delightful
book that I didn't want to put down. I loved the story and the depth of the
characters."*
—Review by Robin Roberts for Once Upon a Romance
4.5 rating on JUDITH'S PLACE, Book Two in
Dreams of Plain Daughters

*"This was another enjoyable story in the Dreams of Plain Daughters
Series. I loved the complexity Ms. Craver wove with these characters and her
storyline."*
—Review by Diana Coyle for Night Owl Romance Reviews
Top Pick, 5 stars on FLEETING HOPE, Book Three

*"Violet and Luke were extremely likeable characters and I felt the highs
and lows they both were experiencing along the way while courting each*

other. . . I always enjoyed Ms. Craver's Amish stories because they each contained characters that were fully believable and you can't help but become invested with each storyline...I feel this is a wonderful series to enjoy in its entirety. I highly recommend this author and this series!"

AMISH BABY SNATCHED

Diane Craver

For my sweet and lovely daughter-in-law,

Lea Craver

Before I formed you in the womb, I knew you.
Jeremiah 1:5, NIV

Be joyful in hope, patient in affliction, faithful in prayer.
Romans 12:12, NIV

Note to the Reader

The Amish community I've created is fictional, but exists close to Wheat Ridge, which is an actual Amish community in the southern part of Ohio. Before I started writing my Amish series, I did extensive research to portray this wonderful faith as accurately as possible. I've used many rules and traditions common to the Amish way of life. However, there are differences between the various groups and subgroups of Amish communities. This is because the Amish have no central church government; each has its own governing authority. Every local church maintains an individual set of rules, adhering to its own *Ordnung*.

If you live near an Amish community, actions and dialogue in my book may differ from the Amish culture you know. The Amish speak Pennsylvania Dutch with variations in spelling among the many different Amish and Mennonite communities throughout the United States. I have included a glossary for the Pennsylvania Dutch words used in this book.

In spite of some of the differences among the various Amish communities, none have electricity in their homes, and they don't drive vehicles.

Pennsylvania Dutch Glossary

Ach: oh
Aenti: aunt
appeditlich: delicious
boppli: baby
bopplin: babies
bruder: brother
daed: dad
danki: thank you
dat: father
Dietsch: Pennsylvania Dutch
dochdern: daughters
ehemann: husband
English/Englischer: not Amish
fraa: wife
freinden: friends
froh: happy
grandkinner: grandchildren
grossdochdern: granddaughters
gut: good
in lieb: in love
kaffi: coffee
kapp: prayer covering
kind: child
kinner: children
mamm: mom
Onkel: uncle
*rumspringa:*running around; time before an Amish young person officially joined the church, provides a bridge between childhood and adulthood.
schee: pretty
schweschder: sister
wunderbaar: wonderful
ya: yes

Chapter One

As Chloe Parrish leafed through a magazine in the doctor's waiting room, she glanced at Beth Byler, an Amish woman. She'd briefly met the young brunette last week at her aunt's restaurant. She wasn't working that day, but had taken her aunt's little son, Tyler, with her to eat lunch there. Instantly, she knew why her aunt had introduced her to Beth. She wanted her to have a connection to another female close to her age.

She sighed, putting the magazine back on the table next to her. What a summer this was turning out to be . . . dull and no friends. She couldn't complain to her parents or siblings, because they'd shrug and remind her that the best solution for her was to continue living with her aunt. Pregnant and stuck in Fields Corner for the whole freaking summer. Living with Aunt Angela and Tyler wouldn't be as bad if her boyfriend, Logan, hadn't gone backpacking in Europe. After high school graduation, she was supposed to take off with him and several other friends, but instead she got pregnant. Now the plan was for her to have the baby and start college in September. That could only happen if she gave her baby up for adoption.

Logan shocked her when he hadn't canceled his trip abroad. She'd expected more from him, and had assumed he'd want to spend the summer with her. For months, he'd told her how much he loved her. Her eyes filled with tears, thinking how everyone had deserted her. Her mother the oncologist and her lawyer father explained it was better for her to leave their home in Cincinnati to visit her aunt. Her father's sister, Angela, needed her to watch Tyler while Grandma Parrish was away. She'd shocked the family when she decided to travel. True, Grandpa had been gone for three years, but she had never traveled any until now.

But I know the real reason they want me away. My family is ashamed of me for getting pregnant. I've never felt like I belonged to this super-perfect family. I know I wasn't planned. Mom thought she was done having kids. She'd already had a wonderful daughter and son.

Feeling a hand on her arm, Chloe glanced up at Beth standing next to her. She noticed Beth's blue eyes filled with concern for her.

"Chloe, are you okay? You look so sad."

Chloe gave a quick nod. "It must be my pregnancy hormones." There wasn't any point in complaining to a happily married woman about being single and pregnant.

Beth took a chair next to her. "I know what you mean. One moment I'm happy and the next I feel like crying. It's hard on Henry. He's my husband and he's so attentive to me."

"That's sweet, though, that Henry cares a lot about your feelings." Logan sure wasn't thoughtful about her needs. Sure, it could be because they both had college goals and hadn't planned on having a baby together until many years in the future. Still, he hadn't hesitated about leaving her for the summer, and that was one thing she couldn't forget. If they had been married, would he have been more caring during a planned pregnancy? When she'd broken her ankle during basketball, he'd given her lots of attention and come to her house a lot to bring her little surprises. You'd think a pregnancy was a bit more of a big deal than a broken ankle.

"*Ya.* Henry worries too much, but I guess it's to be expected, since this is our first *boppli.*"

With many Amish people living in the area, Chloe had quickly learned the meanings of some of the frequently used Pennsylvania Dutch words. "When are you due?"

Rubbing her belly, Beth said, "The middle of next month. What about you?"

"Lucky you with only a month left. I'm not due until mid-August." Chloe wished her baby was due in June instead of August, so that she wouldn't have to go through another two months of pregnancy. Maybe it was a good thing Logan wasn't around to see how huge she'd gotten suddenly. Being tall and long-waisted had helped at her high school graduation. She hadn't popped out much, even though she'd been almost six months pregnant.

Violet Robinson entered the waiting room. "Hello, ladies. Beth, I'm ready for you. Chloe, you won't have to wait long."

"It's okay. I'm early." Chloe patted her stomach and smiled. "For some reason, a little person's kicking woke me up."

Violet said, "Maybe you can take a nap this afternoon."

Chloe doubted that, because she had to get six-year-old Tyler. He'd spent the night with one of his friends.

Beth stood. "Would you like to have a lunch with me after our appointments?"

"That sounds like fun. I have to get my cousin, but it's not until the afternoon." *Having lunch with someone my age sounds like fun,* Chloe thought. *Actually, it'll be the only bright spot in my whole day.*

Chloe liked that Violet took her blood pressure, checked her weight, and asked her questions during each prenatal visit before seeing Dr. Foster. Violet would soon be a certified nurse-midwife and would be allowed to do the home births herself in the Amish community. Even though Chloe wasn't going to have a home birth, Violet seemed to understand how she felt. The senator's daughter told her to feel free to call her between visits if she had any questions.

She hadn't called Violet, but maybe sometime she would. Just to have someone to talk to might help ease her mind about giving birth. She couldn't talk to her mom about what it would be like. It had always been difficult to have meaningful conversations with her mother. Violet had been assisting Dr. Foster in the home births while the previous midwife took some time off to care for her new baby. While waitressing in her aunt's restaurant, she'd heard from several Amish women how caring and considerate Violet was as a midwife. At first Chloe wondered if Violet gave her special treatment because she had worked for her aunt a year ago, but that probably wasn't it.

It had been horrible what happened at her aunt's restaurant when Violet worked there. While dating Luke King, an Amish buggy maker, Violet took a job at the restaurant to be near her boyfriend. Her mother, Carrie Robinson, had grown up in an Amish family, so she decided it'd be good for Violet to live in a house without electricity for the summer. Violet's father, Senator Robinson, agreed, and hoped this would discourage Violet from becoming Amish. He expected his daughter would give up seeing Luke and return to college after her summer job ended. Aunt Angie said people were surprised that Violet survived a hot summer without air conditioning in the house.

Unfortunately, Eric, a science major like Violet, wanted more than a simple friendship with her. Although there hadn't been any serious relationship between them, Eric had fantasized that there could be more. He became violent when he realized Violet loved Luke. He held Violet hostage in the restaurant, and the shot Eric meant for Luke hit Violet instead. It was horrifying when Chloe saw it on all the news media. At the time, Senator Robinson had been considering a run for the presidency of the United States, so it was big news that his daughter had been accidentally shot. A policeman killed Eric during the confrontation.

While waiting her turn to see Violet, Chloe took her smartphone out of her purse. *I might as well text Logan how I have a lunch date. I won't tell him it's with an Amish woman yet. Although I doubt he'll be jealous if he should think a cute guy asked me to lunch.*

* * *

While sitting in a paper gown on the edge of the table in the examining room, Beth complained, "I wish I could've kept my clothes on. Dr. Foster hasn't done a pelvic exam since my first visit. I don't see why he might today."

Violet shrugged. "He might not, but he mentioned checking the baby's position and wants to see if the growth is right for your due date. Just general stuff like that. I thought it'd be easier if you have a gown on instead. He also talked about scheduling you for an ultrasound."

"I hope not. That'll be another expense for us." When Beth saw that look in Violet's eyes she got whenever money was mentioned, she said in a hurry, "I don't want you to pay for it. I can tell you were going to offer."

"Well, I can if that is the reason you don't want it. But there's nothing to worry about. You're doing great. And you said the baby is active. But be sure to call if the baby seems less active than usual."

Beth grinned at her future sister-in-law. "You look cute in your blue scrubs."

Violet frowned as she glanced away from the computer screen. "Thanks, but don't tell your dad I'm not wearing my Amish clothing in here. I assisted Dr. Foster in the birthing center early this morning, and I didn't have time to change before appointments."

"Of course I won't tell him. You haven't joined the church yet anyhow."

"I know I haven't, but my instructions start soon." Violet sighed. "It won't be much longer and Luke and I will be baptized."

Beth's mind swirled with worry at the sound of Violet's voice. *She doesn't seem thrilled about becoming Amish*, Beth thought. Leaning forward, she said, "You don't sound happy. Are you thinking of not joining our church?"

Shaking her head, Violet answered, "It's not that. I'm afraid your dad will change his mind about me being in Eliza and Adam's wedding. I don't want to slip up in any way and have him hear that I'm not serious about becoming Amish. It's important for me to be in my only sibling's wedding. Adam won't be able to be in my wedding."

"*Daed* already gave his permission. He won't go back on his word. Unless he hears you wore a bikini to go swimming." Beth remembered that Eliza's mother had an inground swimming pool in their backyard.

Violet giggled. "I definitely won't be wearing a bikini. Working at the florist shop has definitely made you more outspoken. It must be the Englishers at the florist shop infiltrating your mind."

"I did enjoy the interaction with the customers at the shop. I hated quitting." Beth hadn't wanted to quit her job, but she knew Henry was uncomfortable with her still working while pregnant. One reason she'd wanted to get married at age eighteen was to get freedom. Although she loved her father, he refused to allow his daughters to work in town. It wasn't fair when her brother had a buggy shop. Whenever she'd mentioned it, her *daed* said that Luke's customers were Amish.

Violet's brown eyes narrowed. "I didn't know you quit your job. You loved working with flowers. But that's good you did, with getting closer to your due date. I never thought about how with a new baby, you might not have time to do the flower arrangements for our wedding. I can get someone else."

She'd promised to be charge of the table decorations. Violet wouldn't be carrying a bridal bouquet like Beth had made many times for the English brides. Amish brides never carried flowers, but they were allowed to decorate the tables with them. "It won't be a problem for me." Beth patted her stomach. "My baby can go with me when I create your floral arrangements. I already talked to Donna, the owner, and she said I can come in to do your flowers. She would be hurt if I didn't. It's a big deal to Donna that her flowers will be used for a senator's daughter's wedding."

"I'm *froh* you can still do my flowers." Violet got a dreamy look in her eyes. "I can't wait until we get married."

"I'm excited to have you for my sister-in-law and my midwife. *Ach,* I also stopped working at my job last week because I knew if I continued until I went into labor, *Daed* would hit the ceiling. Henry was relieved that I quit. I heard enough guarded hints from him and my mother-in-law how his *bruders'* wives never worked while they were pregnant." Henry's mother, Beverly, hadn't been shy about expressing her opinions on how Beth could use improvement as an Amish *fraa*, and had criticized her working outside the home.

"I'm glad you got to work as long as you did." Violet grinned. "It's good I decided to be a midwife so when I'm pregnant, I can continue working. I doubt your *daed* will object to me delivering babies."

"That's true, *Daed* won't care. He's never said anything about Ada being a midwife. She's married and has *kinner.*" As Beth watched Violet write on her medical form, she teased, "I hope you aren't putting that I'm a bad patient."

"I did the usual and put in your blood pressure and how you don't have any swelling in your ankles, hands, and face." Violet turned her face away from the laptop to look at her. "If you should have an ultrasound, you could learn the gender of the baby. I know Amish don't want to know until the birth, but you're so inquisitive, I thought I'd mention it."

Beth shrugged. "If Dr. Foster wants me to have an ultrasound I guess I'll have to, but it seems logical that I'll have a boy. Henry has four brothers and no sisters. His two married brothers only have sons too. It seems like there's a good chance I'll have a boy. But girls do run in my family."

"Well, you'll know for sure in a few weeks." Violet closed her laptop, and then stood. "Dr. Foster should be here soon. He's running a little late with the morning delivery he had. Also, he has another doctor with him today. He might become Dr. Foster's partner."

"I don't like the sound of that. I don't want to see another doctor." It'd been bad enough when Dr. Foster had examined her during her first prenatal visit. He'd done a complete physical examination, pelvic exam, and a pap smear. Although she liked Dr. Foster, she'd felt uncomfortable, wishing she had a female obstetrician instead. *After that first visit, Violet reassured me that I wouldn't have routine pelvic exams at future prenatal checkups,* Beth recalled. She hadn't, but knew if the doctor had any specific concern during this particular visit, he might. It'd be awkward for her to have it in front of another male doctor. "What do you think of the new doctor?"

"I hope he decides to accept Dr. Foster's offer, because he's open to home births, and he likes the birthing center too. I'm thankful Dr. Foster pushed for a birthing center here in Fields Corner. And having it close to Luke's buggy shop is awesome. I'm hoping Luke and I will live in the apartment above his shop after we're married."

Beth turned her head at the sound of a knock on the door. Dr. Foster entered first with an extremely young-looking male behind him. How could he be an obstetrician? Was Violet wrong? Not likely. She worked closely with Dr. Foster, and he would definitely talk to her about the medical qualifications of a new doctor he was considering for his staff. *Still, he looks younger than Luke. I thought they had to go years and years to medical school. Hopefully, Dr. Foster will deliver my little one. Or maybe I won't need a doctor. Violet delivered Molly's baby Isaac on the side of the road because they didn't have enough time to get home or to a hospital.*

"How's my favorite patient?" Dr. Foster gave her a quick smile.

Beth shook her head at her doctor. "*Ach*, Dr. Foster, you say that to all your patients."

"Beth, I'd like you to meet Dr. Cunningham. I'm hoping he'll join my practice."

"Hi," Beth murmured to the new doctor, noticing his height and handsome looks. *He's at least Luke's height or taller. I'm glad Violet fell in love with my brother before this Dr. Cunningham appeared in her life. If he takes some of Dr. Foster's cases, Violet might also be working closely with the young doctor.*

"Violet, tell Dr. Foster I'm doing great on my weight gain."

Violet rolled her eyes. "I did tell him." Smiling at both doctors, she said, "Beth's all yours now."

"*Danki*, Violet," Beth said.

With her hand on the doorknob, Violet said, "I'll see you later, Beth. Enjoy your lunch with Chloe."

Chapter Two

Beth couldn't believe she was enjoying lunch with an English girl. Sure, she'd had meals with Violet, but that was always with other family members present. And Violet would soon be part of their Plain family anyhow. For years, her *daed* had been strict about no socializing with the non-Amish. With many English tourists in Fields Corner, he worried that his daughters might decide to leave their community to marry someone outside their faith. When Luke started courting Violet, her father was more obstinate about keeping his daughters from seeking employment in town. He was the bishop of their district, and he wanted to make sure all his children remained Amish.

Although Beth could understand why her *daed* felt the way he did about not working in any store or business in town, she had never agreed with it. After marrying Henry, it'd been wonderful to have her job at the florist shop in town. Being married was awesome and gave her power that she'd never experienced before as a single daughter.

And right now, she was going to enjoy every minute of her lunch with Chloe. Even though they were from different worlds, it would be nice to talk about what they had in common—their pregnancies.

"I've never eaten here before. I'm glad you mentioned eating here. And it smells wonderful in here with the baked goodies." Chloe tucked a lock of brown hair behind her ear and grinned. "I might not tell my Aunt Angie I ate here. Or I could tell her I did it for research to learn more about her competitor."

"I'm glad Martha Weaver didn't stop serving breakfast and lunch. I was afraid she would when your aunt opened her restaurant."

Chloe looked surprised. "Why would she do that? There's

enough business for both of them."

"I don't think she'd mind cutting back. When Martha started serving breakfast and lunch, I heard it was so her son Samuel would have a place to eat instead of packing his lunch daily. Also her regular bakery customers complained about there not being any place to eat in town except for Pizza Hut and Subway." Beth sipped her iced tea, then continued, "Martha decided to expand and serve sandwiches and other things. I like your aunt's restaurant a lot too. Henry and I have eaten there a few times."

"One thing my aunt can't compete with is the bakery items, so she buys pies and cookies from Martha. I might forget about calories and order a chocolate pie for dessert. I've been craving something chocolate."

"We should get dessert. After all, we are eating for two." Beth heard Chloe's cell phone vibrate, and knew that meant she got a text. Because Luke and Violet hadn't started their baptism classes, she'd seen her brother texting. He'd been secretive about his cell phone around his family, but Luke knew she wouldn't tell their father.

Chloe put her sandwich on the plate to pick up her phone. "My boyfriend texted me about my appointment. I'll text him back that everything is fine."

While Chloe was busy with her phone, Beth wondered about the boyfriend and why they hadn't married. It seldom happened that an Amish woman became pregnant before marriage, but the few times it did, the couple always married right away. Chloe looked pretty in her blue sundress, and Beth thought it was a shame that Logan wasn't in Fields Corner. He was foolish not to realize the importance of being with the mother of his child. *I shouldn't pry, but it'd be nice for the baby to have two parents. Maybe they are waiting until after their child is born. Some English couples seem to do that. At least Chloe looks happy now. I hated seeing the tears in her eyes in the doctor's office.*

Nettie Eicher, a young woman with dark red hair, stopped by their table with a pitcher of tea.

"*Danki,*" Beth said as Nettie refilled her glass of iced tea.

"Would you like any dessert?" Nettie asked her.

"*Ya,* that sounds good. I'd like peach pie." Beth thought Nettie was pretty, and it surprised her she was still single. Nettie must be around twenty-three or twenty-four, because she'd stopped going to Sunday singings a year ago.

In their district, it seemed at Nettie's age that single women disliked going to the youth activities. It was too bad she hadn't met anyone in their district to marry. Although James Beachy had taken Nettie out for a few dates, nothing came of them. Maybe he'd been too desperate to find a woman to marry, so that his three young children would have a mother again. His wife, Ida, had died from ovarian cancer. Last winter, James came to the florist's shop to buy a bouquet of flowers for Miriam. Ruth Hershberger's younger sister, Miriam, had moved back to Fields Corner after her husband, Joseph, died in a farming accident. Beth wondered if a marriage might occur between James and Miriam.

Nettie's brown eyes were ringed with thick black eyelashes without the aid of mascara. During her brief *rumspringa,* Beth had used a little makeup, which had included mascara because she wanted fuller eyelashes. Fortunately, her father never knew about her wearing makeup, but her *schweschder* Molly had enjoyed criticizing her for experimenting with it. Molly hadn't even known about her sneaking out to wear English jeans and blouses. It'd only lasted briefly, but was fun to wear something other than their Plain clothing with Henry. He'd worn jeans and T-shirts whenever they went to baseball games and movies.

Chloe put her phone back on the table and smiled at Nettie. "Did I hear something about dessert? I'd like to have a piece of chocolate pie."

"Both *gut* choices," Nettie said. "I'll be right back with your pie."

Chloe cleared her throat. "I'm eighteen and Aunt Angie said you were close to my age. I hope you don't mind me asking, but how old were you when you got married? Do Amish get married younger than non-Amish couples?"

"I'm nineteen and Henry's twenty. We celebrated our first wedding anniversary last December. At first, my parents didn't give their approval to us getting married so young, and they wanted us to wait another year or two, but I finally wore them down. Henry and I fell in love at sixteen. I was so *froh* when he offered to give me a ride home after a youth group singing because I already had a crush on him. And many Amish couples are older when they marry. The average age seems to be between twenty-one and twenty-three." Beth wasn't surprised at the question. She didn't look like she was nineteen, and even if she did, some people might still think she was young to be married.

"Since I'm pregnant, I wish my boyfriend had mentioned marrying me, but Logan never did." Chloe finished eating her chicken salad sandwich.

I can't tell Chloe this, but I think it's terrible her boyfriend didn't marry her. She shouldn't have to go through having a baby without a husband. "He might still decide to marry you. There's time before the baby is born."

Chloe frowned. "Logan's in Italy."

Beth's jaw dropped when Chloe said her boyfriend was out of the States. Why would he leave his pregnant girlfriend to go to Italy? "Why is he there?"

"We both planned on going there plus Germany, France, and Spain with our friends before we started college together. I never thought he'd leave me when I became pregnant. And he wanted me to . . ."

Chloe's voice trailed off. "Did he still want you to go with him?" Beth asked.

Chloe shook her head. "I wish he wanted me with him. Instead, he mentioned I could have an abortion."

What kind of a man would tell his pregnant girlfriend to have an abortion? Logan was being selfish and must not want the responsibility of being a parent. *Chloe is better off without Logan, but maybe once he actually sees the baby he'll change his mind and be supportive.* "I'm sorry. You shouldn't have to go through this alone."

"My parents sent me here because they are ashamed of me for getting pregnant. It's their way of punishing me."

"Maybe they thought a change would be good for you, and I'm sure you're a big help to your aunt with working in her restaurant." When Beth saw sadness in Chloe's blue eyes, she realized homesickness was a problem. She couldn't imagine being sent away from her family. "Do your parents live close enough to visit them for a few days before the baby is born? Or they might want to come here to see you."

Chloe shrugged. "My home is in Indian Hill and it's not that far . . . about an hour away. I could drive there. I have my own car. My parents never wanted to have to pick me up after soccer and track practices, so they bought me a car when I turned sixteen."

Beth couldn't believe that Chloe had gotten her own transportation from her parents. Violet had her own car, too, before she had to sell it. But Violet didn't get a car until she was in college, and she had to pay for half of it. "They gave you a lot of responsibility at a young age."

"I never saw them a lot when I lived at home. My mom's a doctor and my dad's a lawyer. I used to see him more than my mom, but he made partner a couple of years ago in his law firm so now I don't see him a lot."

"Do you have any siblings?"

"I have an older sister and brother. The remarkable thing is they both became younger versions of my parents—my sister's a doctor and my brother is a lawyer." Chloe sighed. "I'm supposed to go to college after the baby's born, but I've never cared about going. What about you . . . do you have any siblings?"

"I have four sisters and one brother. My oldest brother, Luke, is engaged to Violet. My oldest sister, Molly, is married and has a little boy. Priscilla, Anna, and Sadie are my younger sisters."

Nettie appeared by their table with their two pieces of pie. "You wanted the peach, right, Beth?"

"*Ya,* please." Beth felt relief that Nettie had brought their food, because she felt lost over what else to say to Chloe about her unplanned pregnancy.

After Nettie gave them their desserts, she asked, "Is there anything else I can get you?"

When they both replied there wasn't, Nettie gave them their bills and said, "Enjoy the rest of your day, and thank you."

Beth put her fork into the pie to break off a piece but couldn't take a bite yet. Noticing the despair in Chloe's eyes made her want to make her new friend feel better. "I'm sorry about your parents and siblings being busy with their careers. When they see their grandchild, I hope they'll make time for both of you. I mean, who can resist a new baby."

"I'm afraid that won't happen." Chloe poised her fork over the pie. "My parents think I'm too young to keep my baby. They want me to give her to a married couple. Mom contacted an adoption agency here in Ohio. I've visited the website, and I've viewed all the information about each interested couple. It's cool how they have short videos of the prospective parents on the adoption site. I've narrowed it to three couples. I plan to meet with each couple soon. I suppose I'll go through with the adoption, but when I feel the baby move I don't know if I can give her up."

"You said her. Do you know you're having a girl?"

Chloe nodded sadly. "When I had an ultrasound, the technician told me it's a girl. Knowing my baby's a girl makes it even more real to me and harder to decide to proceed with the adoption process. The text I received from Logan today told me to decide which couple would be the best for our little girl. I thought maybe he'd want to give some input on the decision I have to make. I want to pick the right couple for my child."

"Some couples in are our district haven't been blessed with children. A friend of my sister's is now trying to adopt two English girls who are sisters. Adoption is a blessing for women not able to have children."

"That's interesting. It never occurred to me that Amish couples might adopt English babies. I hope it works out for your sister's friend."

Beth couldn't imagine Chloe having to give her baby to someone else to raise. But what else could she do? Logan and her family were not being supportive when she needed them the most. Reaching her arm across the table, she grasped Chloe's hand in hers. "I'll pray for you to make the right decision. Have you talked to Violet about it? She's a great midwife and cares a lot about her patients. She might have some good advice."

Chloe brightened, giving Beth's hand a squeeze. "That's a great suggestion. I don't feel comfortable talking to Aunt Angie about it. She's always busy with the restaurant, and when she isn't she spends time with Tyler. I've even thought about keeping the baby, but I haven't been able to express this to anyone close to me. I think God put you in my life for a reason. Thanks for listening to my problems and for praying for me. I feel better having you to talk to about everything. I don't usually open up to others like I have to you."

Although Beth murmured, "I'm glad I could help," she was concerned. *I don't feel like I'm the right person to give Chloe advice. How can I help her make such a big decision whether to keep the baby or to give the little girl to a deserving couple who aren't able to have a child? If I encourage her to give the baby away, will she regret it later?*

I'll pray that Violet can help Chloe with her decision. I'm glad I'm not in Chloe's situation.

"Hey, if you ever need me to drive you anywhere, just let me know." Chloe took a bite of her pie.

* * *

"Don't be gone too long, or you might get bit by mosquitoes," Aunt Angie said.

Chloe stopped at the front door to smile at her aunt. "Mosquitoes never seem to bother me, but I won't be gone long. Have fun with your game."

Her aunt made sure she spent quality time with Tyler whenever she could. This evening, they'd decided to play Chutes and Ladders. Chloe remembered how her nanny, Kelly, used to play board games with her when she was Tyler's age. *Maybe I should call Kelly and ask her what she thinks I should do. She was like a mother to me. She even came to some of my volleyball games. I almost told Beth about Kelly, but I probably already had shocked her enough by being single and pregnant. I'm sure the Amish mothers stay home to take care of their children, and don't hire a nanny for a substitute mother.*

It's odd, in a way, that I was a result of an unplanned pregnancy, and now I'm in the same situation as my parents were. Well, the surprise pregnancy, not the age factor. Mom and Dad thought they were finished with having children, and I'm sure they didn't want me. They never had a nanny for my sister and brother because apparently Mom wasn't a workaholic then.

Exhaling a deep breath, she decided to stop thinking how her parents didn't love her as much as her siblings. It would serve no purpose to ruin her walk by having such negative thoughts.

After she'd walked for a few minutes, her spirits lifted, because it was fun to see how other people were taking advantage of the lovely June evening. It wasn't humid and hot as it'd been the several previous evenings. Children played outside in their yards, and she saw several people walking their dogs. When she was in front of the next-door neighbor's house, a soft breeze carried the scent of roses from their garden. Loretta Swift, an attractive woman in her sixties, was outside watering her flowers. Chloe said hello and waved to her.

With her free hand, Loretta waved back and said, "Enjoy your walk."

"I will."

Aunt Angie had told her that Loretta and her husband had raised their four children in the same Cape Cod house they lived in now. They had no plans to leave because they enjoyed having their grandchildren over for sleepovers on the weekends.

Her thoughts were interrupted when she heard someone behind her on the sidewalk. Turning her head, she saw Dr. Cunningham running. She'd met him briefly during her doctor's appointment. He was a good-looking man with black hair, and his dark brown eyes reminded her of the color of the chocolate pie she'd eaten for lunch. When the young doctor was next to her, he switched to walking.

Dr. Cunningham gave her a broad smile. "Hi. It's nice to see you're getting exercise too. It's a great evening to be outside."

She noticed he had adorable dimples when he smiled. "I used to run a lot before"—she stopped speaking to point to her belly—"this happened." Embarrassed that she'd mentioned her pregnancy, she quickly asked, "Do you live around here?"

"I'm staying with Dr. Foster and his wife for now. He's trying to convince me to stay in Fields Corner, so that I can become a partner with him."

"I suppose if you like small towns, it should be a good fit for you. Are you from a small town, Dr. Cunningham?"

"No, I'm from Cleveland. And you can call me Tony."

"I guess you must be a Cleveland Browns fan, then."

"You got that right. Are you a Bengals fan?"

Her foot hit a rough spot in the sidewalk, and she swayed against Tony. Immediately, he put his arm around her. "Hey, it's okay if you root for your hometown football team."

"Sorry, the sidewalk's uneven and caused me to lose my balance." She didn't want him to think she had purposely tried to make a romantic pass at him. With his good looks, she supposed females throwing themselves at him had happened before.

He removed his arm. "Are you getting tired? I thought maybe we could stop and get an ice cream cone. UDF isn't very far from here."

"I don't know. I already had pie today, but I do love ice cream."

"You didn't eat a whole pie, did you?"

She laughed. "Of course not."

"That's good. And I don't think even if you had, it would hurt you to have a cone too. You don't look like you're in your last trimester."

"Thanks. I'm glad I don't look as big as I feel. Hey, which college football team do you like?"

"I love Ohio State football. In fact, I'm a big Buckeyes fan and usually go to a couple of their home games each season."

"Right answer. I love them too. I'll get a cone with you since we are both Ohio State fans."

"That's good we have something in common."

His grin was infectious, and she grinned back at him.

Was Dr. Cunningham flirting with her? Or Tony, rather? Glancing at him again, she caught Tony staring at her in a way that could have been mistaken for romantic interest. *What's wrong with me? Of course he isn't interested in me romantically. I'm a pregnant teenager. He's probably lonely like I am . . . being away from home is hard.*

One thing she knew was it felt nice to have a good-looking guy wanting to spend time with her. Logan sure hadn't stuck around to be with her this summer. She also was glad that Tony hadn't done a pelvic exam on her today. It would be too embarrassing to eat a cone with him if he had.

Now that I'm thinking about my condition, I definitely don't want Tony to be the doctor to deliver my baby.

Chapter Three

Chloe had three brightly colored folders next to her laptop on Aunt Angie's dining room table. Inside the folders were the home studies of the couples interested in adopting her baby. Well, they were also the ones she'd selected based on what she'd liked about each couple. It'd been time-consuming reading so many home studies and watching several videos of the prospective parents for her baby. *But time is one thing I have plenty of have these days, since my family and Logan seem to be doing fine without me. I'm glad the agency does these thorough home studies,* Chloe thought as she opened a pink folder.

Aunt Angie put a hand on her shoulder. "How is it going? Do you feel a stronger connection to any couple?"

Chloe liked how Angie wore her blonde hair short. *Will my baby have blonde hair or brown hair like me?* she wondered. Her mom and sister both had brown hair, but her brother and dad were both blond. With her finger, she tapped a pink folder and said, "I like this couple for several reasons. One is because Ashley and Jason are both teachers, so they should have time in the summer to spend quality time with my baby."

Aunt Angie sat on a chair across from her and pulled the pink folder closer to her. After glancing at the picture of the couple for a moment, she said, "They look older."

"Ashley's thirty-eight and Jason's thirty-six."

Her aunt shrugged. "Really? I thought maybe they are in their early to mid-forties. Being older could be an advantage because they might have money saved."

Chloe nodded. "That's true."

"You should ask them what their plans are for the summer. Some teachers have jobs or take graduate classes during the summer to increase their wages."

"I'll have to ask them what they plan on doing about raising a child. Maybe one of them will even take some time off from teaching." Chloe rubbed her forehead. "That won't be good if Ashley and Jason both start back at school in August when I have my baby. Their lesson plans shouldn't be as involved, though."

"Are they elementary schoolteachers?"

Chloe shook her head. "No, they are both high school math teachers. I'm thinking that's good without either having to grade essays. My language arts teachers in high school complained how it took more time to grade book reports and other papers."

Aunt Angie scanned the top paper. "There is definitely a lot of information in here about the prospective parents."

"The adoption agency does a very detailed home study report, and it serves as a recommendation that a family is suitable parents for a child. A licensed professional prepares each home study. I think it's a social worker who does it, and she or he includes all kinds of stuff, like: proof of identity, income, health, criminal history—"

"Criminal history?" Aunt Angie said. "I wouldn't think any criminals would be allowed to adopt."

"I haven't seen any with a criminal background. All the ones I read said that they have not been arrested for any crime."

"That's a relief."

"Where was I? Oh yeah, the report includes character recommendations and biographical information about each family member." Chloe opened a lavender folder. "I especially like this couple. Maybe it's because I have a lot in common with Karen. She played volleyball in high school, and she even coached for several years."

"Is she a teacher too?" Aunt Angie asked.

"No, she's a realtor." Chloe slid the folder to her aunt. "I'll give you the folder so you can look at it too. Jeff's a manager at a Fortune 100 financial and insurance company."

Aunt Angie stared for a moment at the photos. "Karen's pretty. How old is she?"

"Thirty-seven, and Jeff's thirty-nine." Chloe grinned. "I know it seems like I'm picking older couples, but wait until you see my next couple. Kristin and Shane look super young." Opening a blue folder, Chloe gazed closely at the final couple. She liked how they looked, and loved what they had written about their life. But what had made her seriously consider them was the fact they had a little daughter. It would be great for her baby to have a big sister, and one so close to her age. "You have to take a look at all their family pictures with their little daughter, Evie. She's two years old, and Kristin is a stay-at-home mom, which I especially like. She was a registered nurse before she had Evie. Shane owns a construction business."

"That sounds good. Your mom will probably like that Kristin was in healthcare."

"Kristin had a high-risk pregnancy with Evie and a difficult recovery from the delivery. The doctors said that another pregnancy would be way too risky."

Aunt Angie peered closely at the family picture of Kristin, Shane, and Evie. "They're an attractive couple, and their little girl is adorable."

Chloe continued in an eager voice, "I like how they wrote about their neighborhood being kid friendly, and that it has a great school district. Their house is close to a community park and swimming pool. Many of the neighborhood families go to the pool and park. They have lived in their house for six years. It's cool how they have a patio with a gazebo where they host frequent cookouts with their friends and families."

"That reminds me of the gazebo in your backyard. I thought it was wonderful when Richard had it built for your mom. They used to be so much in love."

Chloe raised her head quickly to stare at Aunt Angie. "What do you mean? They still love each other." Her dad had always taken time to do a lot with her mother. Chloe knew that they still reserved one night a week to go out to eat together. Of course, they never took her on those nights, which was understandable. *I probably got pregnant during one of their date nights.*

"Oh, right." Aunt Angie shrugged. "I just meant he wanted to do something special because of their love for each other."

"You scared me for a moment. I thought maybe my pregnancy is causing them to fight." *Yeah, right, like they would take time to fight about me.* She didn't want to think about her absent parents and wanted to continue talking about Kristin and her husband's perfect lives. "In the summer, they also enjoy being outside on their patio swing. And in the winter, Kristin mentions how they enjoy the fire pit because they make s'mores and drink hot chocolate. I can see my baby girl growing up and having a lot of family time with this couple."

I never had this closeness with my parents, Chloe thought sadly. *They were too busy working. Both parents put hours into their careers. No wonder they didn't have time for me and won't for their first grandchild. Although I think Dad wouldn't mind me keeping my baby, Mom convinced him that was not a practical solution. He always listens to her. For being a lawyer, he doesn't seem to have any backbone when Mom argues with him. But I guess he likes to keep peace in the family, so shuts up instead of having a continued argument.*

"I like all these couples a lot. What am I going to do?" Chloe asked.

"You should meet the couples in person and have them come to the restaurant or even here to the house. I think meeting and spending time with them should help you to decide. I noticed that Ashley and Jason live in Cincinnati while Karen and Jeff live in Dayton. Where does this last couple live?"

"Kristin and Shane live in Columbus."

"I loved Columbus when I went to Ohio State. There's a lot to do, and the people are friendly." Her aunt gave her arm a reassuring squeeze. "I know you'll make the right decision. I better scoot upstairs to read to Tyler."

"I want my baby's adoptive parents to spend time reading to my baby . . . like you do with Tyler."

Aunt Angie frowned. "Didn't my brother or your mom ever read to you?"

"They seldom did; they were busy with their demanding careers. My nanny, Kelly, read to me a lot, so that was nice."

"I was hoping my brother would cut down his hours, but sometimes I think he feels a need to compete with your mom. She has saved many lives with her cancer clinic. It must be hard to live with a well-known oncologist. Pamela's success rate with cancer is huge. And I guess that's the reason they . . ." Aunt Angie paused, looking nervous.

"What were you going to say?"

Aunt Angie cleared her throat. "I was just going to mention that they were too consumed with their jobs, and that was why they didn't read to you."

Chloe didn't think that was what her aunt wanted to say, but it probably wasn't important to ask her again. "My mom has made a difference in the lives of many people. Because of her efforts, many people have been cured of their cancer. I'm proud of her and my dad. They are both amazing." Except when they ignored her, but she didn't need to sound spoiled and mention anything more about feeling neglected by her mom and dad.

"Maybe you should ask each couple if they plan to hire a nanny. I'm sorry you spent more time with Kelly than your parents. I hope Tyler doesn't feel like I'm not spending quality time with him. It's hard managing a business and being a single mother." Aunt Angie took a deep breath. "Maybe our separation is working. Jim's been sober for eight months."

"I know it's been hard, but your tough love forced Uncle Jim to get help for his alcoholism."

"Mommy, are you coming?" Tyler yelled.

Aunt Angie grinned. "And my child speaks." She stood and walked to the foot of the stairs. "I'm coming, Tyler. I was talking with Chloe."

"Don't forget my drink of water."

"I'm glad you reminded me. I'll get it now."

As her aunt walked by the table to go to the kitchen, Chloe stood and hugged her. "You're a fantastic mother. Tyler's blessed to have you. And I'm thankful each day that you took me in this summer."

Her aunt hugged her back. "I love having you here. You've been a big help with Tyler and the restaurant. You are always welcome here. And your baby is welcome, too, if you should decide to keep her."

After her aunt left the dining room, Chloe stared at the pictures of Kristin, Shane, and Evie again. They had posted many pictures of them with family and friends. A wedding picture of Shane and Kristin was included; she noticed Kristin was a little overweight in her gown. Shane had light brown hair and Kristin was blonde. Little Evie had her mother's blonde hair. *I definitely want to meet these couples.*

Her cell phone vibrated and she saw it was her mom calling. She experienced a flash of disappointment that it wasn't Logan. She picked up her phone and said, "Hi, Mom. What's up?"

"How was your doctor's appointment? Is everything fine?"

Instead of Chloe getting a warm feeling when she heard her mother's voice, she knew there was a definite reason for this call. Her mom never called just to say she missed her or loved her. "Did Aunt Angie tell you about my appointment?"

"No, Logan's mom did. Apparently Logan mentioned it to her."

"Did he say anything else about me? Like maybe he should be a man and come back to the States to spend time with his pregnant girlfriend?"

"I agree with you that Logan should have canceled his trip abroad, but now you know that he might not be the one for you. Besides, you and Logan are much too young to get married."

"It would've been nice if he had at least asked me."

Her mother cleared her throat. "Do you think you would have accepted? You couldn't support yourselves, let alone a newborn."

"Oh, I don't know. Our house is so gigantic that you and Dad might not have realized we were living with you."

"Chloe, I've explained to you before why we bought such a large house. We can have a lot of the fundraisers right in our home to raise money for my cancer clinic."

Chloe sighed. "I know. It's not just to show how successful you and Dad are, but also to get rich people with big pockets to give to the clinic. And Dad brings his lawyer associates to dinner parties. I get it."

"Have you chosen a couple yet for your baby?" her mom asked in a sharp voice.

"I've narrowed it down to three couples."

"That's progress since the last time I checked with you. Where do they live?"

"Dayton, Cincinnati, and Columbus."

"That sounds perfect. Since they aren't too far away, you could come home next weekend, so that we can meet all three couples in person at a restaurant."

Chloe felt nervous, so gave a little chuckle. "Not all at once, I hope."

"Of course not. I thought maybe you could come home on Thursday and rest. Then one couple per evening."

"A social worker has to be present when I meet with each couple."

"We could do all of them on Saturday or Sunday, then, and space them a few hours apart."

"I'll think about it." Actually, her mom's suggestion sounded like a good plan, but she needed to give it more thought before committing to it. *I wish Logan could be present to meet all of the couples. I don't know if I want my parents there anyhow. I should be mature enough to interview the possible future parents of my baby.*

"You shouldn't wait. You only have two months left before the baby's due." Her mother paused for a second, and then continued, "Could you email me the couples you have selected, so I can familiarize myself with them? I'll share the information with your dad too."

"Sure, I'll email them as soon as I get off the phone." Chloe hated to ask her mom, but had to know something. "Even though I'm probably giving the baby up for adoption, would you be interested in coming to the birth? And Dad could be in the waiting room and see the baby after she's born. I'd like you both to share the first moments of my baby's life."

"Oh, Chloe, I'm glad you want to include us. I wasn't sure you would want us to be there."

"So is that a yes?" Chloe wanted to hear her mother affirm she'd be present. In the past, she wouldn't show up for Chloe, and would apologize how busy she'd been at the clinic. Always, she had scanned for her mother in the crowd of spectaculars at her volleyball and track events, but Dr. Pamela Parrish seldom attended. Her dad and siblings did a few times. Even though they were not close, it would be nice to have her parents at the birth of her child.

"We'll be there unless something happens and we can't get away."

In a soft voice, Chloe said, "Mom, this is your first grandchild. I know I'm not married so it's not the perfect occasion you would prefer, but I can't go back and change anything."

"I know you can't. I realize you aren't happy with us for sending you away for the summer, but Angie needed help with Tyler. She told me you're doing great in the restaurant too."

"I am. Maybe I'll stay in Fields Corner and continue being a waitress."

"Chloe, I hate it when you get flippant with me. But you're definitely being more responsible than Logan."

"I still love him. I'm hoping he will cut his trip short and come back home. If we weren't going to the same college, I don't know what I would do. I miss him so much."

"Your dad and I have been thinking maybe you should come home after the baby's born. You can start college the second semester instead. You might not feel up to starting college so soon after childbirth."

"I want to start when Logan does. He and I have always planned on doing this."

"We can talk about college when you come home. I need to take a call from one of my nurses. Be sure to email me the information about the couples you're interested in for the baby. Bye, Chloe."

"Bye, Mom."

What is up with Mom telling me I can skip the first semester? Before she was anxious for me to have the baby and get back home in time to leave for college.

She attached the adoption files to an email and hit send to her parents. Then she decided to send them to her sister, Andrea and her brother, Carter. Maybe her sister would decide to adopt her baby. She'd heard Andrea complaining that life was unfair because she and her husband hadn't conceived yet. They had been trying for a year to get pregnant. Their next step was to see a fertility specialist.

It didn't seem fair about her sister. *Andrea probably works too much, and it's because of stress that she can't get pregnant. But I don't dare tell her that.*

After closing the folders, she looked through her photos saved on her laptop. Recent ones were of her high school graduation. Her eyes filled with tears as she gazed at Logan's handsome face.

She loved his wavy brown hair and gray eyes. With his arm around her shoulders, they looked like a happy couple.

If I keep the baby, maybe Logan will fall in love with our little girl, and in a few years, we can get married. And Mom and I might become closer if she gets a chance to be a grandmother. There will be a new bond with me being a mother too.

The baby gave her a few hard kicks. Glancing at her belly and the movement of her sundress, she said, "My little baby girl. Even if I give up raising you, I'll love you forever." As tears ran down her cheeks, Chloe prayed, "Please, Lord, help me in making the right decision for my baby."

Chapter Four

Beth removed her good dishes from the cabinet shelf. Her china set had been an engagement gift from Henry because it wasn't the Amish way to give engagement rings. Instead, china or a clock was given at the time of this romantic event. She loved the small blue floral accents on the dinnerware.

Henry opened the back door and showed her a bouquet of flowers he'd picked for her. "Will these do for the table?"

Grinning, she nodded. "*Ya.* You did good."

"What time is Chloe coming?" Henry asked, setting the flowers next to the sink.

"Around five o'clock. She had to work at the restaurant today, so will go home first to change her clothes." Beth opened the oven door and peeked at her meatloaf. "I hope she'll like what I fixed for supper."

"Your meatloaf is always moist and delicious."

"I hope she likes the peanut butter pie I made for dessert. Maybe I should have made chocolate pie instead. She loved the one she ate when we had lunch together."

"She'll love the pie. I'm glad you made the peanut butter one." Henry took Beth in his arms. "It's nice you invited Chloe, but I wish you wouldn't be concerned about having her here. You don't need to worry that I'll open my mouth and say something wrong." He grinned. "I'll behave."

Beth saw tenderness in Henry's gaze as he peered at her intently. She kissed Henry, and when their lips met, she almost wished Chloe wasn't coming to their house. Having an intimate meal with Henry would be *wunderbaar.* "I was happy that I invited Chloe for this evening until Violet told me about her background. Maybe I should have had it another evening when Violet could have been here too. When I invited Chloe, I hadn't realized she comes from a wealthy background. Violet's brother, Adam, is getting married today."

It'd been a surprise to Beth when her father told Violet she could be a bridesmaid in an English wedding. She supposed it was because Violet hadn't been baptized yet in their church. She imagined the wedding would be impressive, with it being a senator's son getting married.

Henry gently tucked a lock of her brown hair inside her prayer covering. "It's going to be fine without Violet. I guess you think it'd help to have another non-Amish woman present to help Chloe to feel more at ease in our home."

"Violet told me that Chloe's parents own a mansion in an expensive neighborhood. Her mother is famous for the work she's done in the cancer field, and Chloe's dad is a highly regarded lawyer. Chloe doesn't act snobbish or anything, but still, our lives are so different from what she is used to."

Henry gave her shoulder a squeeze. "From what you have told me, I have a feeling Chloe might feel more at home here than at her house."

During their lunch, Beth had given Chloe her phone number and explained to her how Amish didn't have phones in their houses. Beth gave Chloe the times she could be in the phone shanty so they could talk. This past week it had been fun talking with Chloe on the phone. She was glad Chloe had accepted her invitation to come to their house this evening, but now wondered if she should've invited her for an afternoon visit instead. Chloe might be tired after working all day in the restaurant.

Glancing at the wall clock, Beth saw it was four thirty. "I better finish up here before she comes. I'm glad the weather isn't too hot today. Chloe's used to air conditioning."

Beth walked to the sink to fill a vase with water for the flowers. "Chloe told me on the phone about the families she's considering for adoption. She's going to bring their files this evening. What if she asks me which couple I'd choose? I'm sure Violet could help her better in choosing an English couple. Chloe mentioned how one family said they would have a college fund for her baby. She said that was important too. We don't go to college, so I wouldn't even consider that a reason to choose a couple." She carried the vase to the table, placing it in the middle.

Henry frowned at her. "You could tell her to keep the baby. God might not want her to give the baby away. Her family should be able to help her with raising the child."

"Her parents are in favor of adoption, so that's not an option for Chloe."

When she heard a car door slamming shut in the driveway, Beth said, "That's probably Chloe now. Do you think I look okay?"

"*Ya*, you look cool as a cucumber and very *schee* in your dress."

"I don't feel cool. I'm nervous and hope everything goes fine."

Beth left the kitchen to go to the living room. She opened the front door before Chloe even knocked. "Hello, Chloe. Come on in."

Chloe wore a light pink dress with black dots. There was a black collar around the neckline, and it was the first time Beth had seen Chloe in a long dress. Seeing how pretty she looked made Beth happy she had decided to wear a new blue dress that Molly had made for her.

Chloe smiled. "Your gardens are beautiful. I almost went off the road enjoying the view. You must work hard to keep your flowerbeds so perfect. Is your vegetable garden in the back of your house?"

"It is. I'll show my garden to you after we eat. Would you like to see the house now?"

"Oh, I would. I'm glad you invited me. I couldn't wait to be finished at work, so I could get ready to come here. Thanks so much for inviting me."

Henry walked into the living room. "Welcome to our home, Chloe."

"You must be Henry." Chloe extended her hand to Henry. "I'm happy to meet you. You have a beautiful house. Beth told me that you built it yourself."

Beth noticed Henry looked embarrassed. "*Danki*. I had help from my brothers and Beth's *daed*."

"Well, it's still amazing that you and Beth have this beautiful house and property. You're both young yet and have accomplished a lot. It's nice, too, that soon you'll have a baby in your home."

"We're blessed." Beth touched Chloe's arm. "I'll show you the upstairs."

While Chloe walked behind Beth on the steps, she asked, "Could we sit on your porch after we eat? I want to soak in the peacefulness of your farm and gaze at your flowers. Aunt Angie told me I'd be impressed with an Amish house, but I never pictured what an incredible property you and Henry would actually have."

A rush of thankfulness filled Beth that Chloe liked her home. *Now if she likes what I fixed to eat, I'll be even happier.* Beth decided to show her the spare bedroom first. "If you ever want to spend the night, here is our guest bedroom." Beth giggled. "Well, it'll be available until we have lots of children."

"That sounds great to have a large family. You and Henry will be wonderful parents." Chloe glanced around the room. "This is very nice, and a good size for a bedroom."

"I'm grateful to have our own house with a baby on the way. We lived with Henry's parents before the house was finished." Beth watched Chloe as she stopped in front of a framed painting.

Chloe stared at the picture. "This is a pretty country scene."

"My sister, Priscilla, did it. She has such an amazing art talent. She and Noah Hershberger are both great at creating pictures. I'll show you a picture that Noah did when we go back downstairs—I have it in the living room. He gave it to us for a wedding gift. Priscilla and Noah both include people in some of their artwork, but they don't draw their faces."

"Why don't they draw faces?"

"Amish consider posing for photographs to be an unacceptable act of pride, so we don't allow pictures of ourselves." Beth didn't think it necessary to mention to Chloe how her father preached often about pictures being "graven images," and how Amish believed that photographs where their faces could be recognized violated the Biblical commandment, "Thou shalt not make unto thee any graven image."

Chloe nodded. "I've heard that reason for no picture taking, but didn't realize it was true for drawings. That makes sense it would be the same."

"Noah and Priscilla have sold some of their work at our annual school fundraiser."

"When is your fundraiser? I'd like to attend."

"It's the end of August usually. Right before school starts." Beth walked to the doorway. "You have to see our bedroom and the cradle that Henry made. We have everything ready for the baby—sheets for the cradle mattress, diapers, bibs, clothing, and a crib for when he or she outgrows the cradle."

Chloe followed Beth in the hallway, and as soon as she entered their room, she went to the cradle. Touching the wood, Chloe said, "If I keep my baby, could Henry make me a cradle? I know this is a busy time for him with farming, but I'd pay him extra."

"Actually, Samuel Weaver helped him with the cradle. Samuel might have a few cradles for sale." Beth grinned. "They seem to sell fast to English tourists."

Running her fingers over the oak cradle, Chloe said, "Probably because the craftsmanship is excellent."

"We have an antique cradle that was recently given to us. It's a bigger cradle but needs a little work."

Chloe gave Beth a sad glance. "I think it would be great if I could keep my baby, and we could enjoy being new mothers together."

It sounds like Chloe is thinking of buying a cradle and keeping her little girl. Maybe that is God's plan for Chloe and her baby, Beth thought. "That sounds like fun. Are you having second thoughts about adoption?"

Chloe shrugged. "I'm still torn about what to do. Some days I can't believe I'm even thinking about adoption, and other times I can't imagine being a single mom. I'm going to make phone calls this weekend to the couples. I decided to talk to them and see if they might be available to meet with me soon. My mom called the other night and thinks I need to meet them in person. She's right, but I hate to get their hopes up and then change my mind about adoption."

"I'll keep praying for you."

"Thanks. I've been praying too." Chloe walked to the bed and her blue eyes widened. "This quilt is beautiful. I love the dark blue and light blue rings with the white background. Did you make it?"

Beth shook her head. "My mother made it for me. It's called a double wedding ring design, and is a popular one for mothers to quilt for their daughters. They sell quilts at the school fundraiser, too, if you should be interested."

"I'll remember that." Glancing around the room, Chloe pointed to the windows. "The white material you used for the curtains makes the room airy. I bet you made them."

Nodding, Beth said, "*Ya*. I did."

"I know you don't believe in electricity, but I see you have a lamp with a light bulb. I'm guessing it's battery powered."

Beth nodded. "The lamp does have a battery. We use propane and natural gas lighting, but during the night when I have to go to the bathroom . . . you know how often that is with being pregnant . . . I want to switch on a lamp quickly without messing around with propane. It gives off enough light that I can see to go to the bathroom without running into furniture or tripping over something."

Chloe moved closer to the lamp and inspected the shade. "I love this glass lampshade. The Native American design is gorgeous."

"Henry bought it for me. Are you hungry? I am."

"Me too. I ate an early lunch at the restaurant."

After they left the bedroom, Beth pointed to a room that was next to hers. "When the baby's a little older, we'll put him in there. Molly bought me baby monitors for a gift, so that I'll feel safe having the baby in another room."

* * *

An hour later, supper was over and the dishes were done. Chloe had insisted on helping with the dishes, and said it'd be fun to clean up together. While Henry went to the barn to check on the livestock, Chloe and Beth decided to eat their pie on the front porch. Both women sat on rocking chairs with red and white checked pillows on the seats.

"With all my padding in my behind, I'm not sure I even need a cushion on my chair. But this chair is comfy." Chloe closed her eyes as she swallowed another bite of pie. "This is the best pie I've ever had. You have to teach me sometime how to make a crust as flaky as yours."

Beth smiled. "I have to admit that I never saw anyone enjoy my pie as much as you. I'm glad you like it. I almost made a chocolate pie because I remembered how much you liked the chocolate pie at Weaver's Bakery."

"It was delicious too, but your peanut butter pie is better." Chloe glanced at Beth. "I want to return the favor and have you and Henry over soon."

"I'd like that, but I know you're still working at the restaurant, and you have Tyler to take care of a lot. It might be too much for you."

Chloe raised her eyebrows. "Are you kidding? I feel like a slacker after I see all the work you do here. Your house is immaculate, and I can tell you work hard in your gardens. You even hang out your laundry while I toss mine in a dryer. If I did all this, I'd be tempted to order takeout, but you manage to prepare yummy meals like you served this evening. I think I can make one meal for you and Henry."

When a buggy started coming down their long driveway, Chloe noticed Beth looked concerned. "Looks like you're going to have more company."

Beth put her pie on the table between their chairs. She patted her *kapp* and replied, "It's my parents."

"You don't look happy. Is it because I'm here?" She didn't want to cause problems for Beth. Her dad held importance as the bishop in their Amish district, and from what Beth had said, he never wanted his daughters to associate with non-Amish people.

"It's okay. I just wasn't expecting to see them tonight."

Chloe wondered if she should go inside to finish her pie, but that was silly. It'd be good to meet Beth's parents as long as they didn't ask her about her husband. She was glad now that the adoption folders of the three couples were still in her car. *I don't want to shock them that I'm not married. Geez, I'm sure Amish might sometimes have unwed mothers.* She prayed silently, *Please help me not to say anything that might offend Bishop King. I'm thankful to have Beth's friendship, and don't want to cause any friction between Beth and her parents.*

As she finished praying, Chloe noticed Henry leaving the barn, carrying a bucket of water. Beth's father tethered the horse to a hitching post while Henry gave water to it.

While Chloe slowly ate another bite of pie, she watched Beth's mom greeting Henry. Mrs. King's hair was a rich, glowing auburn color. Soon she left Henry and climbed up the steps to the porch.

Beth leaned forward in her chair. "Hi. I'm surprised to see you and *Daed* this evening."

"I wanted to see how you're feeling," Beth's mother said, her blue eyes showing the depth of her concern as she looked at her daughter. "I haven't heard from you all week."

"I'm feeling fine. *Mamm,* I'd like you to meet my friend, Chloe Parrish." Beth looked toward Chloe. "This is my mother, Lillian King."

Beth's mom gave her a warm smile. "It's nice to meet you, Chloe."

"It's nice to meet you too, Mrs. King," Chloe said.

"*Mamm,* would you like a piece of pie?"

"*Nee,* but I'm sure your father will." Mrs. King moved a vacant chair closer to Beth. "I needed to get your father out of the house. He's been edgy with Luke at Adam Robinson's wedding."

"Adam is Violet's brother," Beth explained to Chloe.

"Aunt Angie mentioned Violet's a bridesmaid for her brother's wedding." Chloe realized that Bishop King must not like Luke attending an English wedding, but really, what was the big deal? From what Beth had told her, Luke planned on starting the baptism classes this month, so was obviously committed to their Plain way of life. Going to Adam's wedding was not going to influence Luke to change his mind about joining their church. She personally thought it would've been odd if he hadn't gone to the wedding. Luke should share this special and happy occasion with his fiancée.

"Where are my sisters?" Beth asked.

"They stayed home."

Beth rolled her eyes. "I guess they didn't care to see me and learn how I'm feeling with their niece."

Mrs. King gave Beth a puzzled glance. "What? You know you're having a girl. Did you have an ultrasound?"

Beth grinned at her mother. "I don't know and was teasing you, but I do have a feeling that Chloe and I both will have girls."

"What's this I hear about girls?" Bishop King asked, as he appeared on the porch.

Chloe noticed Beth's dad was a handsome man with a thick head of graying hair.

"Beth mentioned having a girl but she doesn't know yet," Mrs. King said.

"*Daed*, this is a friend of mine, Chloe Parrish."

Chloe hoped she didn't look surprised at Beth saying they were friends. She hadn't expected Beth to claim their friendship to her father, but it was nice she did. She felt the same way about Beth. Unfortunately, she saw the frown on the older man's face, and watched him stroke his gray beard. She murmured hello to the bishop and said the usual "nice to meet you" statement, but noticed he just nodded at her.

"I don't recognize your name. Are you and your husband from around here?" Bishop King asked.

"No, I'm from Cincinnati. I'm spending the summer with my Aunt Angie. She owns a restaurant in town." Chloe stood, not wishing to be asked more questions about her personal life. "Speaking of my aunt, I should leave soon. I'll take our pie plates in the kitchen. Would either of you like a piece of Beth's delicious pie? I can bring it out with me."

Bishop King gave Chloe a small smile. "Y*a*, that sounds good. *Danki.*"

After Chloe went into the kitchen, she exhaled a deep breath. She shouldn't feel this uncomfortable around Beth's parents, but she did. Well, not her mother so much, but her father. *Either Beth's father seemed cool toward me because I'm English or he knows that I'm not married. Fields Corner is a small town and news travels fast.*

Opening the refrigerator door, she removed the peanut butter pie. *I should cut a piece for Henry. He mentioned eating one once he was done in the barn.*

"You don't have to leave," Beth said, coming into the kitchen. "I could tell that my father made you uncomfortable. I doubt my parents will stay long."

"I was going to leave at eight o'clock anyhow. Remember, I told you that Tony wants me to go to a movie with him. I'm thinking I should leave soon so I have time to change my clothes." She'd decided to wear a maxi dress because Beth's Plain dresses were long, but she should wear something more casual to go with Tony to a movie.

"*Ya,* I know, you're going to a late movie. You figured I'd want to go to bed early anyhow. I'm afraid you're right that we don't stay up late because we get up early in the morning."

"After this incredible food, I might fall asleep during the movie."

"Maybe you can call Dr. Cunningham to see if you could go to an earlier movie."

"That's a good idea." Chloe saw Beth's expression still and grew serious. "What is it?"

"I'm surprised Dr. Cunningham would ask a patient out. Are you going to mention it to Logan?"

In the short time since they've become friends, Chloe had realized that Beth wasn't shy about asking questions. "It's not a date. And Tony isn't sure if he's going to stay in Fields Corner and become Dr. Foster's partner."

"I'm going to make *kaffi* to go with the pie. *Daed* loves his *kaffi* even when it's warm outside."

"Does he know I'm not married?"

"He didn't ask."

Chloe slid a piece of pie on each plate. "You make the *kaffi* and I'll take the pie to your father."

"Who's the second piece for?" Beth asked as she stared at the two pieces of dessert.

"Henry."

"*Ach,* that's right, he wanted a piece after he finished his chores."

Chloe put her hands on her hips. "So who's the most flustered now?"

Chapter Five

Cincinnati, Ohio

Before a filled Catholic church, the priest said to Adam and Eliza, "Since it is your intention to enter into marriage, join your right hands, and declare your consent before God and His Church."

After Adam took Eliza's hand in his, he said in a clear voice, "I, Adam Robinson, take you, Eliza Dunbar, to be my wife. I promise to be true to you in good times and in bad, in sickness and in health. I will love you and honor you all the days of my life."

Then it was the bride's turn to say her consent to marriage. "I, Eliza Dunbar, take you, Adam Robinson, to be my husband. I promise to be true to you in good times and in bad, in sickness and in health. I will love you and honor you all the days of my life."

So wonderful they memorized their vows to say to each other, Violet thought. While listening to the rest of the wedding ceremony, Violet's eyes filled with tears. Happiness filled her soul at her brother's commitment to his beautiful bride. Eliza's long strawberry-blonde hair touched her shoulders under the sheer veil.

After the blessing and exchange of the wedding rings, Violet took her seat with the other bridesmaids in the front pew. Eliza's brother, Austin, took his place behind the podium to give the prayer of the faithful. The wedding ceremony would be longer than a Protestant wedding because Eliza wanted a mass like her parents had had at their wedding.

A humorous thought crossed Violet's mind, that an Amish wedding ceremony would not be short either. Of course, the length would not be a problem for her mother, because she enjoyed attending the long church services. Being raised Amish, Carrie Robinson felt comfortable in praising the Lord in this type of religious setting. Although her father had managed to survive many long and boring senate meetings, he seemed to get restless when attending long services.

Everyone responded, "Lord, hear our prayer," to each intercession the best man, Nick, read. At one time, Violet had been in love or infatuated with Nick, and even been jealous when he'd wanted to date her cousin, Rachel. After working with Nick in her dad's office, she realized he wasn't the one for her. She was happy for Nick that he was now engaged to a sweet and pretty woman, Renee.

Violet took a glance at her brother. He was seated in the front next to Eliza. She was proud of his decision to become Catholic last Easter. Even though she was the one to change from her Protestant faith to Amish instead of Luke leaving his church, it was the right decision for her. *But I can understand why Adam wanted to become Catholic before his marriage to Eliza. Being united in faith as a couple in front of friends and relatives on their wedding day was as important to Adam as it is to me.*

Eliza had chosen lavender and ivory for her wedding colors, which were lovely for the June evening wedding. *What a relief that I haven't been baptized yet, and Bishop Amos gave permission that I could be in the wedding,* Violet thought. When Eliza had asked her to be her maid of honor, it meant a lot to her. It was too bad Judith couldn't have been in the wedding party too, because they were such close friends. Eliza had met Judith when she observed her Amish class for her education degree. Because Judith had already joined the Amish church, she couldn't be a bridesmaid in an English wedding.

Once Austin finished the prayer of the faithful, the priest started the Liturgy of the Eucharist. Since Eliza and Adam were seated next to each other in the front, it was easy for the wedding party and guests to see them. While looking at Eliza's elegant white dress with beaded lace, Violet remembered how much fun it'd been to go shopping with Eliza and their mothers. The bridal shop even had champagne and appetizers. She hadn't drunk any champagne because she never drank any alcohol. After her closest friend, Jenny, died from alcohol poisoning in college, she'd made the decision not to drink. Sadness touched her as she thought about Jenny. Her friend had loved life, always eager to help others. Life was unfair to take someone like Jenny already.

Suddenly they were at the part where the sign of peace was exchanged. Violet turned to shake hands with the people around her and they said to each, "Peace be with you."

After communion, the priest gave the nuptial blessing: "You have declared your consent before the Church. May the Lord in his goodness strengthen your consent and fill you both with his blessings. What God has joined, men must not divide. Amen."

Violet prayed silently for her brother's marriage and gave thanks for her new sister-in-law.

* * *

In the reception hall, Luke's jaw tightened as he watched the photographer snap pictures of Violet. She wasn't aware of her picture being taken, and he didn't want to say anything. This would be her last time in an English wedding before she took the kneeling vows. Anyhow, it was the wedding photographer and not a news reporter. It just seemed to him that the photographer should be taking more of Eliza, the bride, than the maid of honor. Although Senator Robinson had decided not to run for president of the United States, a lot of people still had an immense interest in him and his family. The public's admiration of Senator Robinson hadn't stopped like Luke's bishop father had hoped. The Robinsons had managed to keep the news media away from the wedding and reception by allowing reporters to take a few pictures of the wedding party only on the church steps. The weather was beautiful, so it had worked out great taking a few outside shots after the ceremony.

Violet had been relieved that her future father-in-law had allowed her to be in Adam's wedding, because Eliza and Adam wanted her to be part of their special day. They had on purpose scheduled it for June before she became baptized into the Amish church. If they had waited until after her baptism, then she couldn't have been a bridesmaid.

Luke was happy that they were starting their instructions this month to join the Amish faith. Soon after baptism, he would be marrying Violet. That was their plan, anyhow. *I'll feel better when we are husband and wife.*

There won't be a wedding photographer at our wedding. And I hope no reporters, Luke thought. Even though Amish didn't believe in having their pictures taken and never posed for them, sometimes Englishers took pictures of them without asking. And Violet wasn't Amish, so she could wear an expensive English dress as maid of honor. She even wore a necklace and sparkly earrings. True, she'd enjoyed wearing jewelry before she had decided to become Amish. Luke sighed, realizing how pretty Violet looked wearing her fancy English formal clothes and with her face all done up, but he preferred seeing her in a simple *kapp* and plain dress.

I hope this elaborate wedding doesn't put any ideas in Violet's head that she'd rather not become Amish, so she can have an English wedding, Luke thought.

"Hey, Luke. Did you ever see Violet dance before?" Samuel asked.

Luke turned away from watching Violet to look at Samuel Weaver. Samuel's wife, Rachel, was Violet's cousin. Before they were married, Samuel had worried Rachel might leave their Amish faith. During her *rumspringa*, she'd gone with Violet and her Aunt Carrie to Florida to experience English ways. On her return to Fields Corner, Rachel had decided to join their church. Samuel's brother, Jacob, and his girlfriend, Judith Hershberger, were also seated at the round table with Luke. Violet had a seat at the bridal table.

Luke shook his head. "No, I haven't. Why do you ask?"

Rachel pointed toward the dance floor. "The disc jockey just announced that she's going to dance with Adam. I think it's sweet they'll have a brother-sister dance. I got tears in my eyes when Adam danced with *Aenti* Carrie. It was touching to see mother and son dancing together."

Great, now Violet's dancing, Luke thought, watching Adam lead Violet to the middle of the floor in front of several hundred guests. "I'm not sure about her doing this. Hopefully, my *dat* won't hear about it."

Judith patted his arm. "It's okay. She didn't take the kneeling vows yet."

When he noticed that Violet had a smile on her face, Luke said, "You're right. She's not Amish and can dance. If my *dat* lectures me and Violet, I'll tell him that we haven't even started our classes." It was *wunderbaar* that Violet was still English and got to dance at her only brother's wedding.

It'd been *gut* for him to delay his own baptism, so he could date Violet. She was beautiful inside and out. He couldn't imagine life without her, and knew God's plan for his life had been to meet Violet. Fortunately, she'd survived the bullet shot meant for him. A past college acquaintance, Eric, mistakenly thought he could win Violet's love if Luke were out of the picture. Something good came out of that situation when Violet saw how the Amish from his district parked their buggies in front of Angela's Restaurant, where she was being held hostage by Eric. She was touched by their support.

Slow music continued for a couple of minutes, then suddenly changed to a fast beat. Adam and Violet broke apart and their dancing movements caused the guests to loudly clap their approval. *Well, this will make the video,* Luke realized. Violet had mentioned to him that the ceremony and some of the reception would be taped by a videographer that Eliza had hired. He couldn't help himself, and grinned. "I didn't know Violet and Adam were this talented."

Samuel chuckled. "Adam told me what they planned. They spent time working on their dance."

"I didn't realize Adam and Violet were going to do this. They are both great dancers. I'm impressed." Judith smiled. "Eliza only told me that she and Adam wanted to do a slow, romantic dance when they took the floor. I loved how he swirled her around and did a cool dip. It was nice they had the bridal party join them after a few minutes for a fast dance."

"I wish *Daed* could see this." Rachel flipped the strings of her head covering over her shoulders.

"Ruth told him to come, but he didn't want to leave her alone with Leila. I can see why Ruth didn't want to bring a new baby. So many people and lots of noise." Judith blinked her blue eyes. "Oh great, where's Matthew and Noah? I don't see them anywhere. We better make sure they're behaving."

Luke glanced around until he saw the Hershberger twins. They were across the room talking to their older brother, Peter, and his wife, Ella. "They're with Peter."

It'd been a huge surprise when his former teacher, Ruth Yoder, had married Violet's Uncle David. Then recently the couple had a new baby daughter. David and his first wife, Irene, had been blessed with five children, including twin sons, Matthew and Noah. When Irene suddenly died from a heart attack, it'd been hard on the whole family. When Ruth fell in love with David, she was thirty-five, had never married, and had been a teacher for years. Luke remembered Ruth had planned to marry Daniel Beachy at age twenty. Unfortunately, he was killed in a buggy accident a month before the wedding.

After their dance, Violet kissed Adam's cheek.

"Violet's headed this way." Samuel's eyebrows shot up. "Hey, Luke, maybe she's going to ask you to dance with her."

Luke shook his head. "I don't know how to dance."

"I'm sure you could move your feet around on the dance floor enough for a slow dance," Rachel said. "It'll be a nice memory for you two before you're baptized."

Shrugging, Luke said, "I'll pass on the dancing."

"When is our driver coming back to get us?" Jacob asked, looking uncomfortable. "I'm ready to go home."

Judith frowned at her boyfriend. "This will be the only time we attend an English wedding reception. Adam's our cousin and Luke's *dat* seemed okay with us attending."

Luke nodded. "He's not thrilled about Violet being a bridesmaid, but I think in a way he liked that I wouldn't be the only one wearing plain clothing. I hope there won't be any pictures of us anywhere on the Internet or newspapers."

"Uncle Scott had people at the church doors and reception to make sure no reporters came in." Rachel's eyes widened. "If there are any pictures of us, we definitely didn't pose for them. And I didn't notice anyone snapping ones of us when we left the church."

"That doesn't mean anything. They could've been off in the distance and taken our pictures, but I hope you're right." Samuel sipped his soft drink.

Judith gave Luke a thoughtful look. "I still can't believe how things have worked out. When Eliza came to observe our Amish classes for her college courses, I never would've thought she and Adam would meet and fall in love. But an even bigger surprise is you and Violet falling in love."

Luke took a bite of a pretzel, then smiled at Judith. "I guess Violet couldn't resist a handsome man like myself. By the way, *danki* for taking Violet to the singing that first Sunday. I knew I couldn't help myself as soon as I met Violet. She's an amazing woman."

* * *

Violet decided to make a quick trip to the restroom. After all that dancing, she wanted to check her hair and lipstick. She loved how the beautician had done her hair. It looked great with the one-shoulder bridesmaid dress she wore. As she stood in front of the huge bathroom mirror, she fingered her long brown curls that still fell over her one shoulder. Her hair had remained pulled back in the curly-side ponytail hairstyle.

"Can you believe Violet is going to marry that Amish guy?"

Hearing the woman speak from one of the bathroom stalls made Violet stop fussing with her hair. *Obviously the woman doesn't know I'm in here*, Violet thought. *I don't recognize her voice.*

"Well, they say love is blind," answered another woman. "I think she decided to become a nurse-midwife to try and fit in with the Amish community, and to keep her smartphone. She's my best friend. I hate that she wants to become Amish. I don't see it lasting between Luke and Violet. She'll end up being miserable becoming Amish. I can't see her living without electricity. Geez, she's a famous senator's daughter."

Violet bit her lower lip, feeling hurt when she realized it was her friend, Mandy, talking about her. *I thought Mandy understood how I've already adjusted to living a plain life, and it makes me happy. And she thinks I became a midwife so I could keep my cell phone? Really, she has no clue how much it means to me to participate in the miracle of life when I assist a mother in bringing her baby into the world. Has Mandy ever listened to me telling her how meaningful my life is now?*

"I agree. How can she leave her family to marry an Amish man?" the woman asked Mandy.

"That's another thing," Mandy said in an irritated voice. "Violet won't be able to be in my wedding when she joins the Amish church. And, of course, I can't be a bridesmaid in her wedding."

The woman giggled. "You could become Amish too."

"Like that's going to happen. I'm not going to drive a horse and buggy and wear old-fashioned clothing to be in Violet's wedding. That would be too weird. Luke should be the one changing his life to fit in Violet's world."

A toilet flushed, but Violet remained standing by the sink. *I'm not going to rush out the door to save them the embarrassment of seeing me. I need to tell Mandy how wrong she is about everything she said.*

Violet watched as someone opened the door of the last stall. When she saw it was her friend, she said, "Hi, Mandy."

Mandy's face flushed a bright red. "You look beautiful, Violet. I love how your hair looks. It's cool how the hair is in a twist in the back and then pulled to the side of your face."

Violet crossed her arms across her chest. "I heard your conversation. I thought you understood how I don't have a problem becoming Amish. It feels the right thing for me to do. I've prayed about it."

Mandy stared at her for a moment as she stood next to a sink. "Okay, I guess you heard our conversation. Of course I didn't realize you were in here. Maybe it's good you heard what I said. Why can't Luke change his faith? You have to give up so much to become Amish. It doesn't seem fair to me or to others."

"I couldn't ask Luke to change even if I wanted to. He's a buggy maker."

"That's another thing. He only has an eighth-grade education. You not only have a college degree, but you will soon be a nurse too." Mandy pressed down on the handle of a soap dispenser and rubbed the soap between her hands.

As Violet watched Mandy rinse her hands, she thought about mentioning how a true friend wouldn't talk behind her back, but decided not to. "Our education differences don't matter to either of us. And by the way, Luke has more than an eighth-grade education. He has a high school diploma. I don't think of Luke being inferior, and he's extremely intelligent. I'm not making a mistake. I love Luke with my whole heart. I thought you understood how much it means to me to be Luke's wife . . . and not just his wife, but his Amish *fraa*."

When Violet saw the other woman standing behind Mandy, she moved away from the mirror and pointed to the nearby sink. "Here, you can use this sink. I'm leaving now to spend time with Luke." Glancing at Mandy, she continued, "You might want to be careful about talking in restrooms the next time; you never know who might overhear your conversations."

Chapter Six

Fields Corner, Ohio

Amos sat beside Lillian on the sofa. "I wish Luke would get home."

"It's getting late. There isn't any point in staying up until Luke gets home." Lillian squeezed his shoulder. "We can talk to him tomorrow morning about the wedding."

"I won't be able to sleep until he's here. You know I'm not *froh* that he's at an English wedding. I like Violet, but I still wish at times Luke had fallen in love with someone from our Plain community."

"I wanted that, too, but we have to accept Luke's choice for a wife. He's not a teenager with an infatuation but a grown man." Lillian removed her prayer covering.

Although he knew his wife was right, it still was hard to believe that his only son was going to marry Violet Robinson . . . a senator's daughter. She'd grown up in a completely different world than theirs. How could two people with such different backgrounds make it as *ehemann* and *fraa?* "I wonder now if I gave up too quickly. Maybe we should've insisted he break up with Violet."

Lillian's blue eyes narrowed. In a sharp voice, she said, "*Nee,* that would have been a huge mistake. Have you forgotten how Violet saved our son's life?"

"She wouldn't have needed to take the bullet if they hadn't been a couple. That unbalanced man wanted to get rid of Luke because he was with Violet." Amos exhaled a deep breath. "I'm just afraid that after they are married, Violet will resent giving up her English life to be Amish. She might think it's romantic now to become Amish. Once they join our church and are married, there's no turning back. If they do, we will have to shun them."

Lillian gave him a frustrated glance, and he knew she had more to say on the topic. *I should've kept my opinion to myself. Of course, Lillian won't want me to think a marriage with Violet won't last for our son.*

"We can't think this way. We need to have faith this won't happen." Sitting on the edge of the sofa, she continued, "Violet has embraced our way of life. She's a midwife and loves delivering the babies in the Amish homes. She's been wearing plain clothing—"

Lillian held up her hand when he opened his mouth to protest, but that wasn't going to stop him from commenting. "She's not always wearing Amish clothing. I'm sure she didn't when she went to the pre-wedding stuff, and, of course, today she wore an English dress. She can't switch back and forth between our simple life and the English one when she's married."

Lillian removed her hairpins, and her long hair fell down on her back. "*Ach*, Amos. She won't switch to English clothing again. Do I need to remind you that Luke and Violet haven't started their instructions yet? Adam and Eliza had their wedding this month on purpose so Violet could be a bridesmaid. You need to take this worry to our Lord in prayer. In Matthew 6:34, it says: 'Take therefore no thought for the morrow: for the morrow shall take thought for the things of itself.' And, 'Cast they burden upon the Lord, and he shall sustain thee.' That's from Psalm 55:22, in case you've forgotten that verse."

Amos watched Lillian run her fingers through her auburn hair, and thought how she still didn't have any gray in it. God had blessed him with this *wunderbaar* woman who wasn't afraid to quote Scripture to him when needed. Even a bishop needed reminders from the Bible when worry overtook his soul. "You're right. I needed to hear those verses from God's Word."

Lillian smiled. "After Luke and Violet get married and live with us, you'll see how everything will be *gut*."

He nodded but still had doubts. It wasn't just the clothing issue, but Violet would have to live in a house without electricity for the rest of her life. True, she'd been living in the house her mother had bought from Ruth Yoder, and Violet seemed to have adjusted. He hadn't complained about Violet and Luke going to the Reds baseball games and going to movies because his son was still in his *rumspringa*. "I'm glad Violet and Luke will start their baptism classes soon. Then all this foolishness with doing English things will stop."

Lillian took his hand in hers. "I know you were disappointed that they didn't get baptized last year, but it's going to happen soon."

He gave Lillian's hand a squeeze. "After Violet was shot and she decided to become Amish, I told her and Luke I could catch them up with the rest of the young people in that class. Once she made this decision, I hoped she'd follow through instead of waiting longer."

Lillian laughed. "Amos, that was only a little over a year ago. Violet was wise to wait to be sure about her decision. Besides, she's been busy taking courses to be a certified midwife and working at the new birthing center in Fields Corner."

"That reminds me of Beth. Soon we'll have another grandchild to love." Amos decided to get his wife's input about Beth's new friend. Something about that Chloe made him uneasy. "What did you think of Beth's English friend?"

"She was sweet." Lillian grinned. "Either she was being polite to jump up to get your dessert, or you made her so nervous that she wanted to get away from you."

"I think she felt guilty around me because I'm the bishop. She's in the family way, except apparently doesn't have a husband or parents. I know why you wanted to visit Beth and Henry this evening. You were trying to get my mind off of Luke and Violet."

"Did Luke come home yet?" Sadie asked upon entering the living room.

Amos smiled at his youngest daughter. That child loved her sweets, and he knew why she was anxious to see Luke. She hoped to get a piece of wedding cake. Luke never forgot his youngest sister, and enjoyed indulging her with little treats. "I'm not surprised you're still up. I know how much you like cake, but it's *gut* tomorrow isn't a church day."

Sadie kissed his cheek. "You know me too well, *Daed*."

"You need to get back into bed," Lillian said. "It's too late for you to still be up."

Sadie clapped her hands when Luke opened the front door, carrying a fancy box. "Is the cake in there?"

"*Ya*. But you better ask *Mamm* if you can eat any now." Luke grinned at his mother.

Lillian shrugged. "*Ach*, Luke, you know it'll be easier to have Sadie eat a piece now."

Although he hated questioning Luke about the English wedding, Amos was curious about it. Had Violet said anything to Luke about how nice it would be not to have an Amish wedding? He wondered if Senator Robinson would mind not escorting his only daughter down the aisle. A lot of major differences existed between an English wedding and an Amish one.

Lillian took the box from Luke. "Come on, Sadie. Let's go to the kitchen. I'll give you a piece of cake and a glass of milk."

Before Sadie left the living room, she gave Luke a hug. "*Danki*, Luke."

"You're welcome." Luke removed his black felt hat and placed it on Sadie's head. "Put this on the peg for me, short stuff."

"How was the wedding?" Amos asked. "Did the Hershbergers go?"

Luke nodded, sitting on the sofa. "*Ya, Dat*. The Amish outnumbered the English."

Amos's eyebrows shot up. "*Ach*, how could that be with an English bride and groom?"

Luke chuckled. "I was kidding you. I suppose when Violet and I get married we could have more English guests."

"That's not going to happen. Look how many Amish friends we'll have attending. Violet will have all her Amish relatives, plus she's already helped Dr. Foster deliver several babies. I'm sure these families will want to witness your marriage vows." Amos stroked his gray beard. "We better say something to Scott and Carrie how we only have so much room. I hope they aren't planning on inviting too many from their English side." *Why couldn't Luke have fallen in love with a nice Amish woman?* Amos thought again. Was that expecting too much of his only son?

Sometimes he wondered if he shouldn't have moved to this area when David did. They'd been childhood *freinden,* and both had decided to go where farmland was cheaper. If he'd stayed back with his parents, then Luke wouldn't have met Violet. *But if I hadn't moved to Fields Corner, I never would've met my Lillian. I'll have to trust God and hope that Luke isn't making the biggest mistake of his life by marrying Violet. She seems to fit in with our Plain community, but will it last? Will she be able to make it through the baptism classes and accept our faith? I hope so, because Luke wants Violet to be his fraa.*

* * *

After Luke read a few chapters of a book to Sadie, he kissed her on the forehead. "Sadie, this is a good place to stop reading. I'll read longer to you tomorrow night. It's late."

"Did you have fun at the wedding?"

"*Ya.* It was a nice wedding."

"I can't wait until you and Violet get married. It'll be fun to have her live with us." Sadie yawned noisily and covered her mouth.

"You better get some sleep. *Gut nacht,* short stuff."

"I'm making a surprise for your wedding gift. I hope you'll like it."

"I'm sure I will," Luke assured her.

As he left Sadie's bedroom to go to his, he thought how simple and sweet Sadie's life was. Being nine years old was a nice age when you just had to worry about getting your chores done and attending school. Sadie could enjoy life without worrying about supporting a family.

When Sadie had mentioned Violet living in their house after the wedding, Luke wasn't sure that would happen. Although many young Amish married couples lived with their parents before they could afford to move to their own house, Luke knew Violet's dad might think badly of him. He'd think Violet shouldn't have to live with her in-laws in their house. Scott had questioned him before if he could make enough money as a buggy maker. The reason he'd decided to get his high school diploma was to show Scott he could self-educate himself and obtain more than an eighth-grade education. But Luke realized it probably wasn't enough for his future father-in-law.

Everyone in the Robinson family had higher education. Adam, Scott, and Violet all had college degrees. Someday Adam would finish his medical schooling and be a physician. As part of the Robinson clan now, Eliza also had a degree and was a schoolteacher. Even Carrie had completed two years of college, so she could resume being a teacher's aide. *I don't plan on going to community college because it won't make a difference for me.*

Removing his suit jacket, he put it on a hanger and thought, *I don't need more education to be a farmer and buggy maker. I just hope my lack of a college education won't matter someday to Violet's dad.*

Then there was his *dat*. After Violet saved his life, his *dat* seemed to understand how much Violet meant to him, and even said that God must want them to be together. *Although my dat and Scott have accepted us being a couple, I don't think they are happy about it. I'm sure both wish that Violet and I had never met each other.*

After his suit was put away in the closet, a vision of Violet in her bridesmaid dress flashed through his mind. Later in the evening, she had seemed irritated about something. He never got to ask what was bothering her before he left with Violet's relatives. A driver with a van had driven to the church and stayed in Cincinnati to take them all back home to Fields Corner.

Had Violet regretted committing to the Amish way of life? Was she thinking how nice it'd be to have an English wedding instead . . . like Adam's?

Chapter Seven

"Did you like the movie?" Tony asked, opening the passenger door for Chloe.

"I loved it. Action films with a bit of romance in them are my favorite." She laughed. "Didn't you notice I was on the edge of my seat?"

Before closing the car door, Tony nodded. "I'm glad I didn't give you the bag of popcorn to hold, because it probably would've ended up on the floor. You practically jumped out of your seat a couple of times."

After Tony slid in on the driver's side of his black Mazda, Chloe wondered if she should ask him why he'd taken her to a movie in the first place. The ice cream cone was a spur-of-the-moment thing when they were both out walking, or rather Tony had been running until he slowed down to walk with her. She'd told Beth how it wasn't a date, but he did text her about going to the movie with him. And why would he be interested in a pregnant eighteen-year-old anyhow? Oh no, did her mom know about Tony, and had she put him up to spending time with her? Was he in Dr. Parrish's pocket? Maybe her mom had offered to pay off his college debt, and in return, he was to encourage her to put the baby up for adoption. Her mother was a control freak, and Chloe could see her doing something underhanded like bribery. But it seemed impossible that her mother would even realize another obstetrician was here in Fields Corner.

After driving for a few minutes on the interstate, Tony glanced at her. "Are you tired? You've been quiet. I don't think I told you that you look pretty."

"Thank you." She had spent time switching her top a few times, trying to find one that was flattering to her pregnant belly. She'd finally decided on a blue one, and liked how it looked with her jeans. "You look nice." *Actually, Tony looks hot, but I don't feel comfortable saying it.*

When Chloe heard her smartphone vibrate, she removed it from her clutch purse, glancing at the screen. "I've gotten a text from my boyfriend, Logan. I'll text him back later."

"Maybe he'll come visit you soon. That'll help pass the time for you."

"I wish, but that's not going to happen. Logan's in Europe. We both planned to backpack together this summer before starting college. I never thought he'd go without me." She hated sharing how Logan had deserted her with Tony because it made her feel like crying.

"I'm sorry. He should have canceled the trip and been here for you."

"Exactly. It disappointed me a lot that he left. I hope he doesn't meet someone and forget about me while he's away. Now my mother wants me to wait to start college. Logan and I applied to the same college so we could be together." She stared at Tony for a moment. "Why did you ask me to go to a movie with you tonight?"

Tony turned his head to look at her. "I like you. We both seem to enjoy the same things." He grinned. "Ice cream, especially."

"I do love ice cream. I think I could eat it every day." *Should I ask him if he knows my mother? No, that might be too direct. I'll mention the adoption option I'm considering. If Mom has talked to Tony about adoption being the choice I should make, then he will encourage me to do that.*

"You remind me of my sister. She played soccer."

"I have a sister and a brother. They're older than I am by quite a bit. Is your sister close to your age?"

"Jill's three years younger. She moved to New Mexico with her husband, so I don't get to see her often."

Chloe put her hand on her belly as her baby kicked. Feeling the baby's active movements made her decide to get Tony's feedback about what she should do. "I suppose you've heard that I might put the baby up for adoption."

"I hadn't heard that."

"My parents think I should. Well, mostly my mom's pushing

for adoption. I've narrowed it down to three couples and want to call them tomorrow. I need to meet with them soon."

"You have a difficult decision to make. You said your mother wants you to choose adoption, but what do you want?"

Seeing Tony's gaze upon her, she couldn't help being touched by the compassion in his brown eyes. It didn't sound like her mom had said anything to him about her. What was she thinking? Her mother wouldn't take time out of her busy schedule to convince a young, good-looking doctor to talk their daughter into giving her baby away. That was a relief, because she liked Tony, and enjoyed spending time with him. "I'm not totally sure about adoption. I'm disappointed that my parents don't want me to keep my baby. They don't have any grandchildren yet. I mean, I get why they can't be thrilled that I'm pregnant and single, but I still wish they would want to be a part of my baby's life. I'm scared that if I decide on adoption, I might always regret it. I've always wanted to have children someday. But if I decide to keep my little girl, then it's up to me to give her the best life possible. It's overwhelming to realize I would be responsible for a child for the next eighteen years."

"Would your parents be able to give you some financial support if you decide to keep the baby?"

"They definitely could, but never mentioned helping me financially with the baby." She sighed. "Have you heard of the Cancer Hope Clinic in Cincinnati? It's my mom's baby. She and a few other doctors started it several years ago."

"I've heard of it. So you have a doctor in the family. What does your dad do?"

"He's a lawyer. My brother and sister followed in my parents' footsteps. Carter's a lawyer and Andrea's a doctor."

"I get it now. They think a baby will prevent you from becoming a lawyer or a doctor."

Chloe shrugged. "You might be giving them too much credit. I think it's more they are embarrassed that I'm pregnant. They've always been aware that I'm not interested in the law or medicine." In a rush, she continued, "I don't mean there's anything wrong with being a doctor. I think it's great you chose medicine for your profession, but a nanny raised me, so I see how time-consuming their careers have been."

"I'm sorry your parents weren't around enough when you were growing up."

"Me too. I don't think they planned on having a third child, because there is a big age difference between me and my siblings. Andrea is thirty-two and Carter is twenty-nine. But hey, my nanny, Kelly, was great." She tried to smile because just speaking about her family life, or lack of it, had made her feel like crying. "You have to love your nanny when she loves ice cream as much as you do."

"Chloe, if there's anything you need, I'm here for you."

"That means a lot." Her eyes filled with tears. How could someone she'd just met seem more interested in her and her baby than her own family . . . well, except for Aunt Angie? "My Aunt Angie did tell me that I could stay with her if I decide to keep the baby."

"That's good you have an understanding aunt. Maybe you should try to talk with your parents some more about your feelings."

"I'm going to. Mom wants me to go home for a weekend and schedule the meetings with the interested couples, but I'd rather do it without her. I'm afraid I won't get a chance to ask my questions, and she'll take over the parent interviews." Touching his shoulder, she said, "I bet you wish you'd asked someone else to go to the movie tonight. Someone with a lot less baggage."

"Never. I'm glad you went with me. I didn't have anyone else I wanted to ask."

She laughed. "That's right. You're new in town and you've seen mostly Amish women. Sorry the female population has been limited for you. But there must be someone else besides me."

"Sounds like you are trying to ditch me. I'm enjoying our friendship."

"I'm glad I met you this summer, but I'm just trying to help you find someone close to your age. I think it would be great for you to stay here and become partners with Dr. Foster. It seems the Amish population is growing."

"I'm not sure I want to do any home births, and that seems to be the main choice of the Amish mothers. I—"

Chloe said, "Don't let the home births stop you from taking the job. Violet Robinson will soon be a certified nurse-midwife."

He nodded. "That's exactly what Dr. Foster said. I do like the birthing center, and the nearby hospital is excellent for a small one."

When Chloe saw Tony's frown, she asked, "What's wrong?"

"You said someone closer to my age. How old do you think I am?"

"Actually, you look too young to be a doctor, so I'm not sure how old you are. Violet Robinson would be closer to your age than I am and make a great girlfriend for you. She's beautiful and smart. You have so much in common with Violet, but the problem is she's in love with an Amish guy."

"That's okay, because I'm not interested in Violet." After he turned into her aunt's driveway, he turned off the engine and said, "I'm twenty-seven years old."

"That's not possible."

"I was seventeen when I graduated from high school. I went to a medical school where they offered a combined undergraduate and medical school programs that was only six years rather than the usual eight years. Then I did my four years of residency at a hospital in Philadelphia."

"It is very impressive how you are already a doctor and still young."

"I never dated much while in medical school, so that helped me to stay focused on my studies. While in residency, the hours were long and there just wasn't a lot of time to devote time to a meaningful relationship."

Happiness bubbled inside her about Tony not having time to get serious about anyone, but a twinge of guilt followed. He was a wonderful person and deserved a special woman to share his life with. But for now, it was nice he wanted to spend time with her.

"Thanks for treating me to a movie. I had fun." Chloe glanced down at her belly. "Apparently, my baby girl agrees. She's been extremely active the whole trip home."

"I can tell." Tony smiled when her blouse popped out a couple of inches.

She grabbed his hand in hers so he could feel her baby. After she put his warm hand on her stomach, he scooted closer. She got a whiff of his manly cologne again, and it made her remember what he'd said to her during the movie. He'd whispered to her not to go into labor early. He'd teased her that maybe an action movie was too much stimulation for a pregnant girl.

When his knee brushed against hers, she felt her heart beat faster.

He grinned. "She might end up being a soccer player like her mom."

She raised her eyebrows, noticing his grin remained on his extremely handsome face. "I suppose that's possible. Logan played soccer too."

"Well, it's definitely in her genes, then."

"Logan has never felt her move. Maybe if he did, that would help him to feel like her father."

"I'm sorry Logan isn't as mature about your pregnancy as he should be. Don't give up on him. He might still come through for you and the baby."

"Tony, we have something in common besides ice cream, action movies, and running."

"What's that?"

"It seems we are both at crossroads in our lives. You aren't sure whether you should stay and become Dr. Foster's partner. And I'm undecided whether to keep my baby, or if the right choice is to allow a couple to adopt her."

Chapter Eight

After the Sunday morning service at the Protestant church, Chloe went with her aunt and Tyler to eat donuts in the multi-purpose room. When someone touched her shoulder, she turned and saw Tony.

"Hi, Chloe." Tony grinned. "Good choice. You chose my favorite donuts."

"Hi." Chloe glanced down at her raspberry-filled donut and a Boston cream one. "You caught me. I'm going to work after I satisfy my sweet tooth. I hope I burn off some of these calories."

"Is it okay if I sit with you and your aunt?" Tony asked.

Chloe had noticed Tony in church, so wasn't surprised to see him in the food line. He wore gray dress pants with a short-sleeved shirt and a blue tie. He looked handsome in his church clothes, and it hit her that she'd seen him more often in regular clothes than his scrubs or a lab coat. "Sure. It might just be me at first. It looks like I've been deserted. Tyler went to sit with his friends. I couldn't believe how fast he grabbed donuts and found his little buddies. My aunt left to talk with Violet and Luke. She wanted to catch them before they leave. Luke's going to start giving buggy rides to the tourists. Aunt Angie wants to buy several buggy rides ahead so she can give coupons to her customers for a free buggy ride. Or something like that."

"We should take a buggy ride. I've never ridden in a buggy, have you?"

Chloe shook her head. "I haven't. I'd like to."

"Let's get a place to sit and I'll get our beverages."

"How about over there?" Chloe saw an empty long table close to the coffeepot.

Within minutes Tony had a glass of milk for her and a cup of coffee for himself.

"I was surprised to see Luke in church." Tony took a bite out of his donut.

"Beth mentioned to me that today isn't church Sunday for them. They have church every other week on Sunday at someone's house. They read Scriptures as a family when they don't have church in their community. Luke hasn't been baptized yet, so he decided to attend the service today. Beth said he only went one other time to this church with Violet. I'm pretty sure he's still committed to the Plain way of life."

"I'm glad you filled me in about how they worship in someone's house instead of a church," Tony said. "I need to learn more about my Amish patients."

Chloe took a big drink of milk. She'd gotten up too late to eat breakfast before church, so was thirsty and hungry. At this point, she probably could eat a third donut, but definitely didn't want to appear a pig in front of Tony. "I don't think I'd make a good Amish woman. I heard they have three-hour services." She lifted her glass of milk and asked, "Have you made any decision about accepting Dr. Foster's offer?"

"I'm considering it. I'll make less money here in comparison to a larger place, but I'm enjoying the small-town atmosphere. I noticed houses sell for less in this area, so I like that aspect." Tony picked up his napkin and grinned. "You have raspberry jelly on your chin."

When his fingers brushed softly against her jaw, she felt little tingles. "Thank you for cleaning me up."

"You're welcome. I doubt you could help it. Looks like your roll has a lot of jelly inside."

Wanting to get off the subject of her messy chin, Chloe thought about Beth having baby monitors. "When I was at Beth's last night, she said that her sister bought her baby monitors. I never thought about Amish women having a convenience like this, but they are battery-powered so the monitors don't use electricity."

"That will make it nice for her to be in another room and be able to hear her baby fuss. I'm amazed how hard the Amish mothers work, but seem so happy when they come in for their visits."

She nodded. "I think it's because they get a break from working when they have a doctor's appointment. No offense, but I hate going to the doctor. I won't like going every week during my last month. Maybe I'll get lucky that the baby is really due this month. I guess that won't be good either, since I don't know what I'm doing. I suppose I dislike going to see an OB because I'm single and pregnant. It's a stressful time for me." *How can I tell a doctor how much I hate going to my appointments? Well, Tony doesn't seem to mind, and looks pretty calm while eating.* "I can't believe how I blab everything to you."

"I'm glad you're comfortable talking to me about how you feel. I'm sure a lot of women feel exactly the same way you do, whether they are married or not." Tony put his cup down. His eyes were filled with concern. "I'm sorry about you not knowing what to do about adoption. Are you still going to call couples today?"

"I'm going to Skype with them after my shift ends. I checked with all three couples to see if they were okay with Skyping with me, and they liked my suggestion. My social worker, Lynne, said that was fine with her." She glanced at her cell phone. "I need to go to work soon and go home to change my clothes."

"Do you want me to drive you? I'm on call, but I'm not expecting any emergencies today."

"Thanks, but Aunt Angie should be ready soon. She's not working today, but wants to go in for a couple of hours to check on things. She's taking Tyler with her. The funny thing is even though I messed up by getting pregnant, Aunt Angie said it's been great having me live with her. Grandma Parrish left for the summer to visit friends, and she usually watches Tyler."

Tony looked uncomfortable. *Oh no, what did I say that Tony isn't happy about? I might as well ask him. I haven't been shy around him so far. I shouldn't start now.* "Fess up. What's wrong?" She grinned at Tony. "You might want to work on your expressions. If you look at a woman in labor the way you look now, she'll definitely think something's going wrong with the birthing."

He shrugged. "I was debating whether to tell you that I'm glad I met you. If you hadn't gotten pregnant, you wouldn't have been here. I'm glad we met this summer. But I know it's not the best situation for you with being pregnant and your . . ."

When Tony's voice trailed off, Chloe said in a rush, "It's okay. You can say it. Pregnant and the father isn't around."

"Like I said before, I'm here for you."

"I'm glad you are. I also have someone else in my corner. Even though I sinned, I'm forgiven. I especially liked one of the Bible verses the pastor gave today, Isaiah 40:29. It's an easy verse to remember, yet a powerful one. 'He gives strength to the weary and increases the power of the weak.' That fits me because I feel overwhelmed with my situation, but God gives me the strength to keep trying to be a better person. I know He will guide me to make the right decision about my baby."

Pastor Steve suddenly stood next to their table. "I'm glad you liked that verse. I think the next verses are incredible too. 'Even youths grow tired and weary, and young men stumble and fall; but those who hope in the Lord will renew their strength. They will soar on wings like eagles; they will run and not grow weary, they will walk and not be faint.'"

Chloe smiled at Pastor Steve and murmured, "Wonderful verses."

She was relieved that Tony and the young reverend started a conversation about the Cleveland Indians. Although she liked Pastor Steve's sermons, she didn't want to talk to him about her problems. Chloe knew Pastor Steve was originally from Cleveland, so it wasn't a surprise that was a team the men discussed.

* * *

Late Sunday afternoon, Chloe returned home after her waitress shift was done. When she saw that Logan had called again, she didn't listen to the message, and wondered about the time difference. She had no clue which country he was visiting now, and really didn't care. It was too depressing to hear about all the places he stayed in when she should have been with him. *Well, he just called me an hour ago so it should be a good time to call him back,* she thought.

She sat on a blue chair in the living room and put her feet on a matching ottoman. She loved Aunt Angie's chair; it was made for a pregnant woman. She held the cell phone and waited for him to answer. After a few rings, she heard Logan's voice.

"Is everything okay?" he asked. "I've been worried. You haven't texted me or returned my calls."

"I went to church this morning and then went to work at the restaurant. Some of us have what is called a job."

"Sorry you have to work. I don't see why your parents didn't let you go with me this summer."

Logan had to be kidding. "I'm pregnant with your daughter. Remember?"

"There is that, but you could have traveled with me for a month. Before I forget, everyone said to tell you hi and they wish you were here." He paused for a moment. "Where were you last night?"

"I was invited to my new friend's house. Then I went to a movie."

"Is your new friend female?"

"Beth is one of my new friends. She's Amish and we are both pregnant, except she's happily married." Chloe couldn't resist mentioning marriage to Logan. Things could be better if they were married and getting ready for their baby together. "Her dad is a bishop in their church. I felt a big uncomfortable, so was glad I had an excuse to leave. Tony had asked me to go to a movie with him."

In a sharp voice, Logan asked, "Who's Tony?"

"He's an obstetrician. Get this . . . he's only twenty-seven. He's thinking of remaining in Fields Corner and joining my doctor's practice." Although Logan was enjoying his summer, she was dying to know which country he was in. "Where are you?"

"I'm in London. I wish you were here. You'd love it." After a slight pause, Logan said, "I didn't realize doctors took their patients to movies. You must be bored to go with him to a movie."

"It's the new thing. Patients are supposed to spend time with their doctors." If Logan became jealous of Tony, he might return to Ohio this month.

"I see you still have your sense of humor. I guess he must be single. I don't think you should spend time with him. Maybe he's using you because he's heard of your mother's clinic."

"We're just friends. And Tony didn't even realize my mother was the one in charge of the Cancer Hope Clinic. I think he's lonely. He doesn't know anyone here, and he lives in the neighborhood."

"Since your parents wouldn't give you money to go with me and the others this summer, I wish you could've stayed home. It seems ridiculous to me that you're living with your aunt and working as a waitress. They sure know how to punish you for something that was out of your control."

"Out of my control? What about you? You're responsible too. I didn't get pregnant by myself," Chloe said. She couldn't keep the anger out of her voice, and wished now she hadn't returned his call. *I need to be calm when I Skype with the interested couples.*

"You know what I meant. I take responsibility for my part in getting you pregnant." He sighed loudly. "Maybe if we both had better home lives, it wouldn't have happened. When my parents spend time at home, they fight all the time. And yours are never home much."

"Will you be here for the baby's birth? I need you to be."

"It depends on when you deliver. I have to go a little earlier to college. Since I didn't do orientation yet, I have to get it in before school starts."

"Logan, I want you with me when I have our baby. She needs to come first."

"What is the point? You're going to give her away anyhow. There isn't any reason in bonding with her when we are too young to keep her."

"I'm not sure about adoption. Whenever I feel her kick inside me, I don't think I can give her away."

"You can't be serious. If you keep her, don't expect us to stay together. I love you, Chloe, but I don't want to give up college to raise a baby."

"I never realized how selfish you were until I got pregnant.

Maybe it's a blessing this happened. I wouldn't want to be with someone who thinks going to Europe is the right thing to do. You should have stayed with me this summer."

"That's stupid, Chloe. What did you want me to do? Drive from Cincinnati to see you in Fields Corner?"

"I wouldn't have left home if you had stayed. We both could've gotten summer jobs and made plans for a new life with our baby." Should she mention that he needed to forget about going away to Butler College? They could both live at home and attend University of Cincinnati or Xavier University. UC would probably be the best choice, since Logan thought he might like to become a pharmacist.

"Chloe, I don't want to keep the baby. The best thing we can do is to give her to parents who are ready to raise a child. Parents with an income and a home. We can't give a baby what she needs. With no college degrees, we will make minimum wage and won't be able to take care of ourselves, let alone a baby."

"Mom doesn't want me to go to Butler College. Maybe you could go to UC instead, where they have an excellent pharmacy program." When her phone beeped, she said, "I need to get off here because I have another call. Please just keep an open mind about changing your college plans. Logan, even if we give our baby away, I still need you so much." Her voice cracked and she felt moisture in her eyes. "Bye, Logan. I think it's one of the couples calling. I have to go."

After taking a deep breath, she said, "Hello."

"Chloe, it's Ashley. How are you?"

"I'm fine. I was getting ready to contact you for our Skype session."

"I should've called you earlier that we need to cancel. Things have been hectic lately. Jason and I have good news and bad news."

Oh no, the schoolteachers have changed their minds about adopting my baby. Maybe it's because I haven't fully committed to adoption. "What is it?" Chloe asked.

"I know you haven't decided yet, but we wanted to let you know that we won't be adopting your baby. We're almost one hundred percent sure that we'll soon be parents of a baby boy. We were at the birth a day ago. The mother said she's going to give us her son to raise. As you know, you must wait seventy-two hours after the birth before you can sign the adoption paperwork. The birth mother seems positive that she won't change her mind. I'm sorry, because we were happy you chose us as one of the couples you were thinking of for your little girl. We were honored."

"Congratulations. I'm happy for you both. You will be awesome parents for your new son." She swallowed hard. "I have to be honest that I'm disappointed for myself, but I appreciate you letting me know today."

Chloe asked Ashley and Jason how much the baby weighed and what they planned on naming him. She wanted to be polite and act happy for them, but it was difficult.

What if the other couples had other babies they could adopt before hers was born?

Chapter Nine

After they arrived back from Henry's parents' home, Beth wanted to complain about her mother-in-law, Beverly, but how could she? Being the youngest in the family, Henry was especially close to his mother, so how could she mention that Beverly was at their house too much? When Henry had finished building their house, she'd been thankful that they could move out of her mother-in-law's. Many young married Amish couples lived with their families before they could afford to build a house, so it had been expected of them. *We should have built our house farther away from Henry's parents,* she thought.

Why couldn't her mother have offered to help her after the baby was born? Then when Beverly had said she'd stay with them for a few weeks, Beth could have said that wasn't necessary because her mother would help her. Most people would think it was sweet that Beverly offered to stay twenty-four-seven for several weeks to help, but Beth knew the real reason. Her mother-in-law thought she was incapable of taking care of Henry and a baby. Beverly seemed to think Beth didn't know how to be an Amish *fraa*, so add mother to the mix and her fate was sealed.

I wish I had a dollar each time Beverly mentions how we were too young to get married. Henry and I would have a lot of money from all his mother's negative comments.

After our baby is born, I'm sure I'll hear what I'm doing wrong as a mother. How can I relax and breastfeed our newborn with Beverly looking constantly over my shoulder?

"Beth, did you hear me?" Henry asked.

"I'm sorry. I didn't." Beth turned off the cold-water faucet, and was surprised that her husband was in the kitchen. She knew he'd gone to the barn to feed the livestock. *Hard to believe I didn't notice Henry came in.* She'd been occupied with rinsing the tomatoes.

Glancing at Henry, she continued, "What did you say?"

"The tomatoes definitely should be clean enough now," he said with a chuckle. "Are you feeling okay?"

"*Ya.* I just have a lot on my mind." *Like your mother and how I don't want her around after I have the baby.* Suddenly, she had an awful thought. What if Beverly wanted to be present during the birth? She hadn't mentioned it so far, but that didn't mean she wouldn't.

Henry opened the refrigerator. "You sit and rest. I'll get the cold cuts out and slice bread for supper. We also have a rhubarb-strawberry pie for dessert that Mom sent home with us. She makes the best pies."

Beth clenched her jaw. "I'm sorry my pie-making skills aren't as good as your mother's."

He gave her an apologetic glance. "I didn't say that right. Your pies are the best. You're an excellent cook." He pulled a chair away from the kitchen table. "Beth, you look worn out. Please sit."

"I'll slice a few tomatoes for our sandwiches, but you can do the rest." It was nice, Beth thought, how Amish never cooked a meal for Sunday supper. Quickly, she picked up a paring knife and started slicing a big tomato. "Are you ever scared about us becoming parents?"

After removing a loaf of bread from the breadbox, Henry stood by her. "I'll admit I worry a little about being a father, but I've enjoyed my nephews, so that gives me a little confidence."

Putting the knife down, she stared at Henry. "I don't think your mother thinks I can take care of our baby. I don't see why she wants to stay here all day and night for a few weeks." She wanted to say more, how she'd always felt like Beverly not only wished they hadn't married young, but that Henry had married someone else.

He shrugged. "I don't think she will stay here that much. I'm sure *Daed* won't want her to stay more than a few days."

"Henry, she's been here a lot already. I feel like she's checking up on me to see if I'm doing everything well enough." She gulped, not wanting to say anything to hurt Henry's feelings, but she needed to anyhow. "I wish we didn't live so close to your parents."

Henry ran his fingers through his light brown hair. "What do you want me to do? Tell my mother that we don't want her here? I don't think I can do that."

"I'm already panicking about having a baby. I know women have babies every day, but I'm scared about labor and delivery. And I worry about taking care of a newborn. I remember enjoying helping with Sadie when she was a *boppli*, but that was years ago." She wrapped a prayer tie around her finger, thinking how she had never taken care of small babies or helped new mothers. "*Mamm* helped Molly when she had Isaac while I stayed home to help Priscilla with cooking and cleaning. I wish now I had gone to help Molly with Isaac." Her eyes filled with tears, and she wondered what Henry thought of her. She'd just said how she didn't want his mother around, then claimed she was stressed about taking care of a newborn. *He's going to tell me that I obviously need his mother here to help me with our baby.*

He pulled her into his arms and said tenderly, "It's going to be okay. I'll speak to my *mamm*, but would Priscilla or your mother want to come a few hours a day to help you at first? I can tell my mother you'll have help that way. I remember my brothers' wives always had help right after they had their babies."

"*Danki* for being so understanding. I think Priscilla or *Mamm* will want to help. I'm surprised they haven't mentioned it already."

He kissed her forehead. "Everything is going to be fine. You concentrate on taking it easy."

She had such a sweet *ehemann*. In a choked voice, she said, "Are you sorry you married me?"

Henry stared into her eyes. "*Nee*. I'm glad every day that I married you. You're a *wunderbaar* wife and you'll be a great mother. I love you, Beth."

With Henry's arms around Beth, and his mouth pressed against hers in a sweet kiss, she relaxed. She knew he'd talk to his mother soon. Maybe Beverly would even listen and decide not to spend so much time at their house. Sure, and it was going to snow in June, but she could always hope and pray that Henry's mom would be understanding and realize spending days and nights with them wasn't necessary.

* * *

Today hadn't gone like Chloe had hoped. First, there was the disappointment about Ashley and Jason not being a possibility for her baby. Then Logan's disinterest in anything related to their baby was hurtful to her. After getting off the phone with him, she'd looked at pictures posted on Facebook and Instagram by their friends, showing their smiling faces. *Does Logan even realize how immature it is for him to be with them instead of me and our baby? Logan could have canceled the trip like I had to.*

To get away from his unstable home life, Logan had spent a lot of time at her house during their senior year. As Christians, they'd meant to abstain from sex, but temptation got to be too much with her parents gone a lot. They shouldn't have stayed alone at her house.

I need to get out of the house. It's not good for me or the baby to feel stress about Logan and sadness at losing a couple that might have been perfect for our baby. Walking might clear my head and boost my spirit.

Chloe pulled her hair back into a ponytail and shoved her feet into her pink running shoes, or rather walking shoes these days. She wore shorts and a sleeveless white maternity top so she shouldn't get too hot outside. Today was an extremely warm day with stagnant and humid air. Although her mother had given her money for maternity clothes, Chloe saved it and instead used her work paychecks for her new wardrobe. She'd been frugal and not bought everything new. Buying a few pieces of maternity clothing from a consignment shop had helped with her budget. Learning to be as independent as possible was important to her. She needed to act like an adult. It was too bad she hadn't been more responsible and not gotten pregnant at age eighteen.

As soon as she left the house, Chloe started on a brisk walk. Glancing toward Loretta's yard, she didn't see Aunt Angie's neighbor outside. Then she remembered they were going to watch one of their granddaughters play softball. After walking for ten minutes, she saw Tony ahead of her, stopped by a tree drinking water. "Hey, imagine seeing you," she said when he looked at her.

"I thought I better get in some running."

From his sweaty forehead, she could tell. "I miss running. If you don't mind walking with me, I have some news about the couples I chatted with."

He lifted his T-shirt up, using it to do a quick wipe on his forehead. "Sure. I'd like to walk."

Seeing Tony's abs for the first time stunned her for a moment. His grin made her realize that he knew exactly why she was speechless, and had probably seen her jaw drop at the sight of his bare belly. Did he do it on purpose so she could get a glimpse of his perfectly sculpted muscles, she wondered?

"Geez, let's walk, then," she said, irritated. An OB should not look this hot, especially if he delivered her baby. How could she concentrate on childbirth with Tony in the room? She definitely had to talk to Violet about wanting Dr. Foster. After all, he was really her doctor.

"What's your news?" Tony asked as he closed the spout on his water bottle. "Good, I hope."

"It's not good news for me, I'm afraid. One of the couples is adopting a baby boy. They just received the news. They are the schoolteachers I was impressed with, so now I only have two couples left."

His dark brown eyes met her gaze. "I'm sorry."

"I'm happy for them but keep thinking maybe they were the best couple for my baby." She shrugged. "I did enjoying talking with the other two couples. Although I like a lot about Kristen and Shane, I was disappointed that Kristen doesn't like organized sports like . . . volleyball and soccer. She thinks swimming, ballet, and no competitive sports is the way to go when they are young. Kristen said maybe in high school she can see the girls becoming involved in playing a team sport, but she doesn't want them exposed to any until then."

"Did you agree with Kristen?"

She gave him a light shove. "Of course I don't agree with her. I loved playing sports. And oh my gosh, she has strong opinions. I didn't think I'd ever get her off the topic. I explained how much I loved playing volleyball in junior high. I mentioned how I liked track and soccer too. She said that track meets last forever.

Apparently her brother was a jock and did track, wrestling, and football. Her parents made her go to all of his games and meets."

"What about the other couple? Did they seem like ones you'd like to choose for your daughter?"

Tears pricked her eyes when Tony said "your daughter," and how it affected her so much that she started crying was a surprise to her. Sure, her hormones were haywire right now with the pregnancy, but she was embarrassed to cry in front of Tony.

After she stopped walking, Tony lifted her chin and looked at her face. "Are you crying?"

She nodded.

He wiped away a tear from her cheek with his thumb. "Don't cry. I'm sorry if it was something I said."

"It's silly, but for some reason, I got emotional when you used the words 'your daughter,' and I feel sad about this whole situation. Maybe I should keep her, but I did like Karen and Jeff a lot. They both have a great sense of humor . . ."

He gave her a small smile. "And they both love organized sports, right?"

"Yes."

"If you feel strongly about keeping your baby, then you should."

"Mom told me that it's selfish to keep the baby when there are parents who can't have children, but they have the stability to give a good life to my child." She swallowed hard. "I'm meeting the couples this coming weekend. We're going to meet in Cincinnati at a restaurant and my social worker, Lynne, will be present. We'll meet with Kristin and Shane on Friday evening, then Jeff and Karen on Saturday."

"That's good." Tony grasped her hand in his. "I'm proud of you."

When more tears ran down her cheeks, Tony hugged her and patted her back. "I'd offer to drive you there, but I'm on call next weekend."

"Does that mean you're taking the position?"

"I'm not sure yet, but will make a decision in a couple of weeks."

"Well, I know one thing for certain . . . if you stay, it will be fantastic for Fields Corner to have you as an obstetrician."

"I think you might be prejudiced because I took you to a movie and bought you ice cream."

"Ice cream always helps." She gave his shoulder a squeeze. "Seriously, you always are here for me. Logan should be the one comforting his pregnant girlfriend, but he doesn't want to be with me. I talked to him this afternoon too, and he can't make it to the birth." She buried her head in Tony's chest, thinking how strong and reassuring it was to have close contact with a caring man. "I know it seems crazy I'd want him present when we might give her away, but I just wanted to share this moment with him."

"Maybe he'll change his mind."

Lifting her head, she stared at Tony, wondering if God had brought this sweet guy in her life so she'd have a special friend to lean on during this difficult time. "You know what, you're a blessing to me. It's nice to vent to you." At the sound of Tony's stomach rumbling, she managed a chuckle. "It sounds like you're hungry."

"I am, but then, I'm always hungry. How about we go get a sub and then get an ice cream cone? I haven't eaten since lunch."

"I haven't had anything for dinner either, and I'm at loose ends. Aunt Angie took Tyler to visit with friends."

"We're close to Paul's house, so I can get my car if you don't feel like walking to Subway."

"It seems like it's getting hotter outside. If you don't mind, I think I'd like to ride in your car."

Maybe Tony and I could watch a DVD back at the house after we eat. Should I tell Logan that I'm spending more and more time with Tony? I still love Logan, and Tony is just a friend. But what if Logan has a female friend while he's in Europe? I don't know if I'd like to hear about him spending time with someone else. Well, it's not like I'm going see Tony after I have the baby. I'll keep it to myself unless Logan questions me again.

Chapter Ten

On the last Thursday in June, Violet went to Angela's Restaurant to pick up lunch for Luke. She wanted to see him before she went to Ella's house. She was relieved that her Amish friend and cousin had agreed to go horseback riding with her in the afternoon. It was definitely something she needed to do; she was getting tension headaches on a daily basis. Working at the birthing center and seeing patients at Dr. Foster's office plus attending home births was taking a toll on her. Although Dr. Foster did the actual deliveries, she went to assist the mothers with their labor. She kept the doctor abreast of the progress of the labor during the home births, so he could swoop in at the end. Once she was certified as a nurse-midwife, she'd be allowed to do home births herself in Ohio. She couldn't wait until her graduate school would finally be finished.

Another reason for her headaches might be due to several people telling her it was a shame that her dad had decided not to run for president. She hadn't slept well last night after Mandy had texted her how disappointing it was that her father had dropped out of the race. It was her own fault for looking at her texts before going to bed, but since she hadn't started baptism instructions, she hadn't stopped reading them. Occasionally, she even texted back, but she'd definitely had quit staying connected to her phone all the time. Using her cell phone for her work calls to pregnant mothers and receiving them when they called about their contractions was fine with her. Bishop Amos had given his approval for Violet to keep her phone, as long as it was used for work purposes. She'd been adapting slowly to the Amish world, and one important way was not to spend so much time on her smartphone texting English friends. She smiled slightly that she now referred to her old friends as being English.

Although Mandy's comments at the wedding reception had bothered her, she needed to forgive her friend. It might be time for them to go their separate ways. It'd be hard to lose Mandy as a friend but might be for the best. Mandy's latest comment had made her feel guilty. Knowing her decision to become Amish had deterred her dad from his political ambitions caused her a great deal of pain. She knew how much it meant to him to make the country a better place for everyone.

As she walked up to the counter, Violet saw Jeremy, the cook and Angela's nephew, wave to her from the kitchen area. She was glad he hadn't quit after her hostage situation with Eric and the sad outcome of his death. Although she'd hated what Eric had done to her, Violet was sorry that he had terrified the customers and employees. Isabelle, the young, impressionable waitress, had quit working at the restaurant. Seeing Violet shot and Eric killed by the police had been too much for Isabelle.

"Hi, Violet," Chloe said. "I'll get your order."

"Here it is," Jeremy said, handing it to Violet. He'd left the kitchen to stand beside Chloe.

She handed Chloe a ten-dollar bill and asked Jeremy, "Hey, how is college these days?"

Jeremy grinned. "I graduated from Clermont College and have an associate's degree, but I'm going to UC in August. I want to become a teacher."

Violet knew many people went to the community college for a couple years because of location and lower tuition cost, and then continued at either Northern Kentucky University or University of Cincinnati. "That's great. You'll be a wonderful teacher."

Chloe rang up her order and handed Violet her change. Then the young pregnant woman put her hand on her stomach.

"Are you feeling okay?" Violet asked Chloe.

"My stomach keeps getting hard, but I'm sure it's Braxton Hicks contractions. They aren't painful and are irregular. I've been having them," Chloe answered.

"She's been complaining about them today," Jeremy said, looking worried.

"Have you had more than five of them within an hour?"

Violet asked.

Chloe shook her head. "No, I haven't."

"You should take more breaks and sit down. How many hours are you working today?" *Chloe's young and she might be overdoing it,* Violet thought.

"I'm only working six hours," Chloe said. "I'm glad you came in so I could tell you about them."

"If you start having more in the next hour, call and we'll get you scheduled to see if you are dilating. I doubt you are because it's too early for you go into labor. Having Braxton contractions is normal. Be sure to get enough rest." Violet picked up her bag of food and smiled at Chloe and Jeremy. "It was good seeing you both. I better be going and get this food to Luke."

* * *

"*Danki* for riding with me. I needed to clear my head." Violet turned her head to look at Ella. Her friend loved to ride as much as she did, but with her baby, Elijah, it wasn't always possible to get away. And it was nice to wear blue jeans instead of Amish dresses where no one would see them. Bishop Amos allowed his daughter, Anna, to wear jeans when she rode on their farm, and when she trained their horses, but only when just family was there.

"I'm glad you suggested it." Ella patted her horse. "Daisy was happy to leave her stall. She needs the exercise. And my *mamm* and *daed* were glad to visit and to watch Elijah . . . well, to spoil him. Being their only grandchild, they adore him. I don't even have to cook. *Mamm* said she'd take care of the meal. You should stay and eat with us. You know how my *mamm* will cook too much food."

"I'd love to, but I have plans with Luke. I suppose I shouldn't cancel on him."

Ella frowned. "You don't sound too excited to see your fiancé. What's wrong?"

"I want to see Luke. I miss him when we aren't together."

Ella's brown eyes narrowed as she stared at her. "So what's bothering you?"

"It's about my friend, Mandy. During the wedding reception, I overheard a conversation about me when I walked into the restroom. Mandy was criticizing me for marrying Luke. She didn't realize I was in there when she was talking to another girl. It was hurtful to hear what she said about Luke and me. It seems like I've made several people unhappy by my decision to become Amish."

"That's not important. What's important is how you feel about everything. I take it she mentioned you joining our church."

Violet noticed how Ella's black hair flowed down to her waist. She hadn't bothered with a *kapp* either when she'd changed to her jeans and a top. "*Ya*, she did. But it's not just Mandy. My dad decided not to run for president because of me. I hate that, because he shouldn't be denied this opportunity. He has a great chance to go all the way and to be elected. Dad cares so much about our country and would do a great job."

Ella frowned. "I doubt you're the reason. Your mom was raised Amish, and he still decided to become a senator."

"But she's left her Amish roots for him. I'm leaving the non-Amish world, and a lot of voters would never understand why a senator's daughter would do this. Some people don't care for the Amish. Unfortunately, they can't be accepting of the way the Amish have chosen to live, and have strong opinions." Violet decided not to mention the fact that although some people might respect the Plain people being pacifists, others resented that they didn't believe in serving their country by being in the military.

Ella gave her a sad look. "That's true. Peter and I were going home one night and a bunch of teenagers were in a car and started harassing us. They drove next to our buggy forever, it seemed, and yelled obscenities. They kept blowing their horn too. It was awful because we had trouble staying on the road, and were afraid of an accident. We hadn't done anything to them and gave the boys plenty of room to go around us."

"I'm sorry. Were you able to get their license number and report them?"

"*Nee*. And we never saw them again. No one was hurt, so we didn't mention it to the sheriff. We prayed for them."

If anyone does this to Luke and me while we are traveling in a buggy, I will report him to the police, Violet thought. "On a happier note, I start my baptism instructions next Sunday. It's funny in a way, because I was baptized in the Protestant church when I was twelve. I was happy to take that step in my Christian life. Mom wanted Adam and me to decide when we wanted to be baptized."

"That's wonderful you had that experience." Ella raised her eyebrows. "You know, you can still change your mind about joining our faith. I think it's good you're going to start the instructions and take it from there. I'm sure Luke doesn't want you to become Amish if it won't make you happy."

Violet shook her head. "I definitely want to become Amish and marry Luke. I'm happy with my decision. I just wish others would be more understanding instead of being judgmental."

"That would be nice."

"We probably should turn around soon and go back to your house. I have a couple of mothers who might go into labor soon."

Ella grinned. "Too bad you couldn't have fallen in love with the new doctor. A nurse-midwife and an OB falling in love would have been perfect. But don't mention I said this to Luke."

Violet laughed as she pulled on the reins, turning Murphy back toward the farmhouse. "It is funny that I fell in love with a buggy maker. I think there could be a romance between Tony and Chloe Parrish. I never thought that would happen with the age difference and the fact that Chloe is pregnant, but they have definitely forged a friendship. They make a cute couple."

"Hey, let's race back," Ella said while using her feet to tap Daisy's flanks.

"You're on," Violet yelled as she spurred her horse to catch up with Ella. "I can't believe you think Daisy can beat Murphy."

Chapter Eleven

Cincinnati, Ohio

On Saturday morning, Chloe sat on the edge of her bed, waiting for Beth to answer her call. *Please, Beth, be in your phone shanty.* They had decided on the scheduled time before she'd left Fields Corner. She couldn't wait to tell Beth how the visit had gone with Kristin and Shane. It was funny in a way how she wanted to talk with Beth instead of her previous close friends. They were all enjoying the summer by touring European countries before they started college. She didn't want to call any of them to talk about her baby. How could they relate to what she was experiencing when none of them were pregnant?

Even though Beth was married and from a completely different lifestyle, Chloe had already bonded with the young Amish woman. Maybe God had meant for them to meet and to comfort each other. Beth had never judged her for not being married and had made time for her in her busy life. It was like the Bible verse in 1 Thessalonians 5:11: "Therefore encourage one another and build each other up, just as in fact you are doing."

"Hello, Chloe. Sorry I'm a few minutes late," Beth said in a breathless voice.

"Hi. No problem. I'm glad you made it to your phone."

"Did you like the couple you met last night? How did it go?" Beth asked.

"It went great. I wasn't sure about my mom going too, but she was helpful. We ate at O'Charley's restaurant and I was pleased there wasn't any awkwardness. Kristin's husband, Shane, asked me about Logan. I was glad he wanted to learn more about the father of my baby."

"So do you think this might be the couple you'd want for your baby?"

"Maybe. I did like the fact they are younger, and another plus is that they already have a little girl. I think it's great they don't want her to be an only child. We are meeting Karen and Jeff, the other couple, today, so I'm looking forward to meeting them. My social worker, Lynne, was pleased how well it went last night. Kristin and Shane seem like the perfect couple for my baby."

"I'm glad you decided to meet the couples in person. I guess you feel more comfortable about adoption now."

She felt a lump in her throat. Amazing how one moment she couldn't wait to tell Beth about Kristin and Shane and how awesome they were, but now she was depressed thinking how they might raise her daughter instead of her. Of course, she realized that her pregnancy triggered a wide range of emotions, but maybe she would always regret giving her baby away. Could she raise her daughter by herself? It was obvious her parents thought adoption was the best for their grandchild.

She cleared her throat. "I thought I did, but now suddenly I feel sad and depressed about everything. I wish my parents would give me encouragement to keep the baby. They said if I keep the baby that it will be harder for me to get a college education. I don't care about college. I wanted to go mainly because of Logan, but now my mom thinks I shouldn't go to the same college as him."

"You should tell your parents how you feel. Didn't Aunt Angie say you could stay with her if you decide to keep the baby?" Beth asked.

"She did, but I hate to impose on her. I'll talk to Mom and Dad again about keeping the baby." Glancing around her room, Chloe thought how there was plenty of room for a baby bed and a changing table. "I don't get why Mom is so against me keeping the baby. I can still attend college and take care of a baby. It'll just take me longer. I need to convince my mother that I can handle college on a part-time basis while being a mother. What am I going to do? I keep changing my mind constantly about what I should do."

"You do have a hard decision to make, but you don't need to decide today. Meet the other couple. Ask your parents if they will give you any support if you decide on keeping your baby."

"Thanks for listening and for caring." Chloe thought Beth sounded a little down. *I hope she's not having mother-in-law problems again. I remember her mentioning how controlling Henry's mother can be at times.* "Beth, are you feeling okay? You sound tired."

"The baby hasn't moved today. He's been active all during my pregnancy, so this is unusual."

"Maybe at this point he doesn't have enough room in your womb to move around because he's a big baby. Or it could be he's sleeping to get energy for labor." Chloe didn't want to alarm her more, but she was worried about Beth's baby not being active. She'd be concerned if her baby stopped kicking her. Chloe had planned to tell Beth about her Braxton Hicks contractions she'd been having, but decided it wasn't a good time to say anything.

"That's what Henry said, but Violet told me during one of my appointments that if the baby stopped moving I needed to tell them."

"I'll pray for you and the baby. Hey, I just thought of something—you said the baby is really active at night. Did he move last night?" Chloe asked.

"He moved a lot early in the evening, but not later. I hope nothing is wrong."

* * *

Just as they had with Kristin and Shane, they selected an earlier time to meet before the evening rush started. Chloe's mom asked for a corner table in the back where it would be quieter. Chloe was happy that her dad and mom both came this time, but she felt a bit of sadness about Logan not being there. *You'd think he would want to meet the possible parents of our baby. He's all for adoption but doesn't want to get involved in choosing anyone. Well, I can't think about how disappointed I am about him; I need to concentrate on learning as much as possible about Karen and Jeff,* Chloe thought.

Her mom looked great dressed in gray capris with cute black sandals and a lavender and gray top. Chloe had been surprised when her mom had given her a new dress to wear for today's meeting. The flowered maxi dress her mother had bought was expensive. Chloe was shocked when she'd removed the price tag. Apparently she wanted to impress Karen more than she did Kristin. She'd thought her mom would want her seriously to consider Kristin and Shane to be the adoptive parents. After all, Kristin was a registered nurse, so her granddaughter would receive top-notch care. Not that Karen wouldn't be a good mother too.

I wonder why Mom wants to influence Karen more than Kristin to adopt my infant, Chloe thought. *It could be because Kristin doesn't want her daughter to play on sport teams. Mom always enjoyed going to my sports when I was younger. She missed some of them, but made more of those than my high school ones.*

I hope I look good enough, but I feel huge, Chloe thought. Her baby bump was definitely bigger, and she noticed Karen and Jeff stopping at that spot when they looked at her. *Maybe they wonder if I'll deliver before August. I wish I could deliver earlier, as long as the baby is ready.*

After all of them placed their orders, Karen smiled at Chloe. "Although I enjoyed talking with you on phone and Skyping with you, it's great meeting you in person. Feel free to ask Jeff and me anything. I know this must be a difficult decision. You are a selfless person, and if you should choose us to be your baby's adopted parents, we will be sure to tell her what a wonderful person you are."

Chloe swallowed hard because Karen's words struck a chord inside her. "I'm happy to hear that, and it's great meeting you both. Thanks for making the trip to Cincinnati."

"You probably read on the website how much we enjoy my sister's three children. She and her husband were blessed with two boys and one girl," Karen mentioned to Chloe.

Chloe nodded. "I did read that. That is so nice. What ages are your nephews and niece?"

"Ten, seven, and four," Karen answered.

"I've taken the boys camping," Jeff said with a twinkle in his eyes. "It was hilarious because the boys couldn't stop talking while we fished. Then they worried what we'd eat when we didn't catch anything. I had plenty of food with me to fix."

"Sounds like you had a lot of fun," Chloe said to Jeff.

"Does your sister live in Dayton too?" her mom asked Karen.

Karen nodded. "She's only ten minutes away. My sister, Janie, and I are very close."

Chloe liked Karen's pleasant smile and how she seemed relaxed. It had to be difficult to be in this position of hoping to convince her that she and her husband would be the best ones to adopt her little girl. Karen was pretty in a wraparound black and white dress.

"Karen even asked Janie to be a surrogate for us, but she didn't want to do this," Jeff said.

Karen's eyes narrowed as she glanced at Jeff. "I knew it was asking a lot of Janie and didn't expect her to want to, but we have wanted a family for a long time. It never hurts to ask, but of course I can understand why that was asking a lot of my sister."

"I'm sorry you don't have children, but maybe soon you will." Chloe felt comfortable in making this assumption. Her mother gave her a pleased look. "I've narrowed it down to you and to another couple we met yesterday." Chloe laughed. "You seem to rate a bit more because my mom suggested we come here instead. Yesterday we went to O'Charley's."

Lynne, the young social worker from the adoption agency, put her glass of iced tea on the table. Her curly brown hair brushed against her chin. "The lunch was good yesterday too."

"It was, but Outback Steakhouse is pricier." When her mom had suggested the steak place, Chloe wondered if her mom was more interested in impressing Karen and Jeff. "I'll try to decide soon. I know this waiting has to be tough, and I appreciate you both taking the time to drive here."

"We're glad you are considering us as parents for your baby. And like I said before, we'll be happy to answer any questions you might have." Karen picked up a knife to cut a piece of meat. "This steak is delicious."

"Karen, are you planning on working outside the home if you adopt my baby?" Chloe thought, *I won't mention that Kristin is a stay-at-home mother. I don't want to influence Karen's answer. I want her to be honest.*

Karen hesitated in answering, but after a long moment, she said, "I love being a realtor, but I've waited a long time to become a mother, so Jeff and I have decided that I'll take a couple of years off from selling houses."

Did Karen take her time answering my question because she realizes that my mom always worked while I was a baby? She might not want to offend Mom, Chloe thought.

Jeff chuckled. "The other realtors will be happy for Karen to take time off from the company. She's been the number one realtor at their agency. It's time she gives the other agents a chance to be at the top."

Karen tucked a lock of her black hair behind her ear. "I'd rather spend time taking care of a baby than selling houses. And Jeff makes a great income, so it won't be a problem financially for me to quit."

Jeff grinned at Karen. "I'm glad, because it will be great to go home in the evening to spend time with my wife and child."

Her mom patted her hand. "Chloe asked this because we had a wonderful nanny for her. I stayed home with our older two children, but by the time Chloe was born, I felt I needed to use my medical training."

"Pam has done an amazing job with her cancer clinic." Chloe's dad frowned. "I think it's going to be hard for me not to have a connection with our first grandchild."

"Dad, I thought you agreed with Mom about adoption."

"I did, but I guess now it's really hit me how I won't be a grandfather and how much I might miss it."

Her mom looked concerned. "When Chloe is older, she might have another child. And Andrea and Carter will probably give us grandchildren someday too."

Chloe asked, "Hey, would you like to see a photo of my boyfriend, Logan?" At Karen's quick nod, she pulled her smartphone out of her bag. Touching the screen, she got Logan's picture up and handed the phone across the table to Karen. "I wish Logan could've made it here today, but he's out of the country."

Lynne cleared her throat. "Logan wants to go to college and

has no desire to raise their child, so you don't have to be concerned about him stopping the adoption."

Her mom said, "We want Chloe to go to college, so this is another good reason for her baby to be adopted."

"Logan and I plan to attend the same college." Although she knew her mom wanted her to live at home instead, she wasn't ready to give up on getting away from Cincinnati.

"What would you like to major in?" Jeff asked, buttering a piece of rye bread.

Chloe shrugged. "I don't know."

"You have two great role models with your mom being a doctor and your lawyer dad," Karen commented. "It should help you having firsthand knowledge of their careers when you decide what to major in."

"I'm not interested in the medical field or the law as careers. Maybe it's because my sister is also a doctor and my brother followed in my dad's footsteps and became a lawyer. I want to do something different." Chloe smiled at her parents. "I don't want to compete in your fields."

"Getting a college degree is important, and Chloe has a high GPA, so I think whatever she decides to major in, she'll do great," her dad said.

Chapter Twelve

On Monday morning, Beth went to their phone shanty and called Chloe to tell her that the baby had stopped moving completely. Beth explained, "He moved early Friday evening like I mentioned to you on Saturday morning, then never moved again until Saturday evening. And no movement on Sunday or today."

"I think you should call Violet or the doctor right now. I'm sure they will want you to come to the office today. I can take you to the doctor. I don't have to work today, and Tyler is at his friend's house."

"*Danki*, Chloe. I'll call Violet now. I'll get back to you."

Violet answered on the first ring. "Hi, Beth. I was just thinking about you. How are you feeling?"

"I'm worried because the baby hasn't moved since Saturday evening."

"You need to come in to the office for a non-stress test as soon as you can get here. I'm at the office, so I'll tell Dr. Cunningham that you're coming."

I want to ask Violet what she thinks is wrong with my baby, but I'm afraid to hear her answer. Please, God, help everything to be fine. "Chloe offered to drive me. I'll call her now."

Twenty minutes later, Beth and Henry were in the examination room. She was thankful that Henry was with her. At breakfast, he'd decided not to work in the fields in case she needed him. Violet had Beth lie on the table with the fetal monitoring equipment hooked to her belly. Beth's dress was pulled up so her belly was bare, and Violet put a paper cover over her legs and panties.

After Violet tried several times to find the heartbeat with

constant glances at the non-stress monitor, she said, "I can't seem to get the baby's heartbeat. I'll get Dr. Cunningham. Maybe it's because of the baby's position. Try to relax and I'll be right back."

As the door closed behind Violet, Beth said to Henry, "I'm scared that she couldn't locate the heartbeat. That has to mean something bad."

Henry squeezed her hand. "It's going to be okay."

After a couple of minutes, Violet returned with Dr. Cunningham. He looked at the test and then said calmly, "Let's do an ultrasound."

Immediately, Violet disconnected her from the fetal non-stress monitor. Then she put some gel on Beth's belly, and the doctor started the ultrasound. After looking for a little bit, Dr. Cunningham said, "There isn't any heartbeat. Your baby girl has died. I'm so sorry."

While Beth cried, she heard Henry's sobs. Until it had been confirmed by the doctor, she'd hoped the baby would be fine. In her mind, she had kept thinking that maybe he or she was resting or had run out of room. But then, the baby should still be able to move a tiny hand or a foot a little if low on womb space. Maybe the baby had even moved while she slept, and it hadn't woken her. Now she had to let go of hoping that their baby would be okay. Her baby had died.

Violet quietly removed her paper cover and smoothed Beth's dress down over her legs.

After crying for several minutes, Beth asked Dr. Cunningham, "Why did this happen? Did I do something wrong?"

Dr. Cunningham shook his head. "Beth, you are not to blame. I don't know why this happened. After the baby's born, we can run tests and do an autopsy, but that still might not tell us why she died."

"I didn't know the baby was a girl until now. We expected a boy, since there aren't any daughters or granddaughters in the Byler family." In a choked voice, Beth continued, "She would have been the first granddaughter on both sides of our family."

"That's right," Henry said, putting his arm around Beth's shoulders. "Dr. Cunningham, what do we do now?"

"You can wait until labor starts or, Beth, we can induce you so you won't have to wait." Dr. Cunningham ran his fingers through his black hair. "It seems the longer a mother carries her stillborn, the more depression she has and the longer the grief process takes. If you want labor induced today, you need to go to the hospital. There is another patient I need to see. I'll leave you two to discuss what you should do. Again, I'm very sorry this happened to you."

Violet followed the doctor but stopped at the door. "I'll be back soon."

Leaning her head against Henry's chest, Beth said, "Our poor little infant won't experience life. We'll never have this child to love and to watch her grow into a young woman."

"I know, but she's in heaven now." Henry kissed her forehead. "Whatever you want to do about labor is fine with me. We can wait or have it started today."

"I don't know what to do. I want to talk to my parents first. I never told them I had this appointment this morning, so I'll ask Chloe if she can drive us to my parents' house."

At the sound of a knock on the doctor's door, Henry said, "Come in."

Beth turned her head and saw it was Violet coming back into the room. Stepping slightly away from Henry, she said, "I know Dr. Cunningham said I did nothing to cause our baby to die, but I need to know what caused this to happen. Violet, tell me the truth. Do you think I did something during my pregnancy that caused our baby to be stillborn?"

With tears in her eyes, Violet shook her head. "I'm sure you didn't."

"But you told me to let you or the doctor know if the baby stopped moving. Did you suspect something might be wrong then?" Beth thought it was strange that Violet had mentioned this about the infant's activity, and then soon after, it had happened.

"I never suspected anything was wrong. It's something we tell every pregnant woman." Violet, standing next to a desk, pulled a tissue out of a box. She handed it to Beth. "I wish I or the doctor could tell you why this happened, but we don't know.

Unfortunately, when stillbirth happens, it's a mystery. And you didn't have any medical condition, like being diabetic or having high blood pressure that would've increased your chance of having a stillbirth."

"If this was God's will, then I wish He'd taken the baby during the first trimester. I know your cousin Rachel had a difficult time after her miscarriage, but at least she hadn't carried the baby for months then lost it." Beth couldn't help it—she thought it was mean of God to do this to her and Henry. They deserved to have this baby and not to have it die in her body. Now they might never know what caused it.

What about the next pregnancy? Would she have to wonder if it would happen again? Using the tissue Violet had given her, she wiped her cheeks.

"I'm sad this happened. Dr. Cunningham is heartbroken too. He wanted to talk longer with you, but he had to leave." Violet grasped Beth's hand.

"Dr. Cunningham mentioned we could wait until labor starts or he could induce labor," Henry said in a low voice. "What would be the best for Beth?"

Beth felt Henry's arm tighten around her waist when he asked the question. She knew why he wanted to know what Violet thought, because the doctor had said waiting too long could be too hard on the mother and cause more depression. *Obviously, it will be hard on me whatever I do. What a choice I get to make. I don't care about having labor now. I had looked forward to holding my sweet infant in my arms, but now my dream has turned into a nightmare. I want to escape all these conversations about not having a baby to love. It's not fair this happened to me. I'm a good Christian woman.*

"I don't think you need to decide now. You just learned devastating news. Labor usually will start within two weeks. If it doesn't, then the doctor can use medication through an IV to dilate the cervix and the contractions will begin. I'm not telling you this to influence your decision about what to do, but waiting longer before you deliver will affect your baby's appearance. But I think you need to make peace or come to terms with what has happened before you're induced. You don't need to decide right now." Violet hugged Beth. "You both are in my prayers."

"*Danki,* Violet." Beth swallowed hard and paused for a moment. What she wanted to ask was a hard thing for her, because she still felt shock and confusion about her baby being dead. *Babies are not supposed to die.* "Do you think we should have an autopsy after she's born?"

Violet replied, "An autopsy can be performed if you want."

Henry frowned at Violet. "I'd rather not have an autopsy or testing done, because it seems like it violates our baby."

Violet nodded. "I understand, and a specific cause might still be unknown after an autopsy."

"What will happen with a second pregnancy? Will I have a higher chance of having another stillbirth?" Although she hated asking this question, Beth wanted to know about their risks for the next pregnancy.

"The chances of having another stillbirth are extremely small. Most women give birth to a healthy baby after experiencing a stillbirth. Dr. Cunningham said there's a ninety-seven per cent that a future pregnancy would *not* end in stillbirth," Violet said. "You don't have to worry about this happening again."

In a firm voice, Henry stated, "For some reason, God allowed this to happen with our first child, but I have faith we'll have a healthy baby the next time."

"Even if we have a healthy baby sometime, nothing can replace this one. I wanted this baby."

"I wanted her too."

"I mentioned the autopsy because people might think I did something to cause our little girl to die. And to tell the truth, I feel guilty. I'll always wonder if it was my fault, but I don't see how it could be. I was never even sick during my pregnancy." Beth exhaled a deep breath and suddenly wanted to get out of the building and to talk with Henry alone. Even though Violet had been understanding, she had never lost a baby. Beth couldn't bear to talk any longer to Violet about their baby.

Violet shook her head. "It was not your fault. It's important for you to remember that your stillbirth was not caused by something you did or did not do. If you want, I can also talk to the grandparents. Your family and friends will be a support for you both. And you might want to join a support group for parents who have experienced the death of a baby so you can share your feelings. You will never forget your baby, but you will heal. Healing won't happen quickly, but eventually it will."

After leaving the doctor's office and going to the waiting room, Beth looked quickly to see if Dr. Cunningham had gone to see Chloe, as she was a patient too. Chloe was by herself and stood when she saw them. Maybe he'd left to deliver a healthy baby. Violet and the doctor probably hadn't wanted to cause Beth more sadness by mentioning another woman was giving birth to a live newborn instead of a dead one.

For a moment, Beth felt anger when she glanced at Chloe. She looked very pregnant in her blue maternity top and jeans. *Why didn't God take Chloe's baby girl instead of mine? Chloe is indecisive about what to do. One minute, she plans to give her baby away, then the next, she wants to keep it. And Chloe doesn't even have a husband, so her child won't have a father if she raises the baby. Henry and I would have been great parents. It's not fair.*

"Our baby girl died," Beth said.

Shock registered on Chloe's beautiful face, and her eyes filled with tears. "Oh no, I'm so sorry."

As her friend hugged her, Beth felt guilty that she'd had unkind thoughts about Chloe. It wasn't Chloe's fault that her baby had died.

Henry said, "Beth wants to tell her parents. Could you drive us there?"

Chloe loosened her hold on Beth and nodded at Henry. "Of course."

Once they were outside and walking to Chloe's car, Beth noticed what a beautiful day it was, and even that bothered her greatly. *The sky shouldn't be a brilliant blue. It should be filled with dark, stormy clouds to fit my mood,* she thought.

"Dr. Cunningham said I'm not to blame for having a stillborn." Beth wanted Chloe to know what her doctor friend had said.

Chloe hit the unlock button on her key and, with her free

hand, touched Beth's arm. "I don't know why this had to happen to the nicest couple in the world, but I do know it isn't your fault or Henry's."

"Beth wouldn't even take an aspirin for a headache. She did everything right. My *fraa* was . . ." Henry's voice trailed off, and after he cleared his throat, he continued, ". . . careful during the whole time."

At Henry's emotional comments, Beth cried again. She had the best husband in the world, and he would have been such a good father to their baby.

Henry opened the front passenger door for Beth. "Life is unfair, but we have to trust God, and maybe our baby had something wrong with her and would've faced serious surgery."

"We could have handled a child with a problem."

He kissed her cheek, which surprised her. Henry was like most Amish husbands and didn't show affection in public.

"I don't feel it now," Henry said in a dejected voice, "but I want to believe that God somehow blessed us with this tragic death and good will eventually come out of it."

Beth glanced at her watch and saw it was noon. "My *daed* should be in from the fields to eat his dinner meal."

Chloe got behind her steering wheel and fastened her seatbelt. "I'm glad you're going to see your family now."

From the back seat, Henry asked, "When do you want to tell my parents?"

For a moment, she thought about asking Henry to go by himself, but that wasn't right. She should be with him when they told Beverly and Henry's father, Justin, the news. She wished now that she hadn't complained about Beverly staying at their house when the baby was born. As it turned out, she'd wasted her time being worried about something that now wasn't going to happen. "I guess after supper, if that works for you. Unless we decide to have labor induced."

Fifteen minutes later, they arrived at her parents' farmhouse. Brightly colored flowers surrounded the white frame house. Staring at her family's home, Beth thought how peaceful and lovely everything appeared.

Chloe put a lock of her brown hair behind her ear. "I don't think I should go in. I'll wait out here."

"You can go in with us," Beth said.

Henry leaned forward. "Amos can take us home so you don't have to stay. We appreciate you taking us to the doctor's office and driving us here. Thank you, Chloe."

"Okay, I'll go home, but be sure to call me if you need anything. And if you decide to have labor started, I can drive you."

"I might do that. Pray for us," Beth said.

After they were inside the kitchen, Beth saw her parents and sisters had just finished eating. While glancing around the room, she thought about all the happy memories she had of here. Her *mamm* had taught her how to cook, bake, and can their produce from the gardens. Her daughter would never experience her mother's good cooking. She'd never hear her grandfather preach on Sundays.

I wish I could go back in time and not have this pain in my chest. Telling my loved ones about the baby is going to be hard, but it has to be done, Beth thought.

Her *mamm*, standing, smiled. "This is a nice surprise. Would you like a piece of pie?"

Beth shook her head and Henry said, "No, *danki*."

After Henry and she sat at the table, Beth took a deep breath. "We came to tell you that our baby girl is dead. There isn't a heartbeat. I was afraid something was wrong when the baby stopped moving. Dr. Cunningham also did an ultrasound, and that's when he said the baby was a girl."

Her *mamm's* blue eyes widened with shock, and her father said, "I am so sorry."

"Maybe the doctor made a mistake," Sadie said as her lower lip trembled. "I don't see how it could be true. I was going to help you with the baby."

Beth leaned closer to Sadie and brushed a kiss against her forehead. She hated seeing her little sister looking so forlorn. "I know, and you would've been a big help. I wish with my whole heart that the doctor was wrong, but he isn't."

"I had a cousin, Annabelle, who had a stillbirth," her *mamm* said. "She and her husband didn't know the baby was dead until she delivered. It was their first child. She went on to have six more *kinner.*"

"I know, *Mamm*, you're trying to make me feel better, but I wanted this baby. I didn't want her to die." Beth couldn't help herself, and the tears flowed.

Her *mamm* gave her a hug. "I wish this hadn't occurred. It's a sad time for all of us."

"I'm very sorry that your baby died. It's a great loss," her *daed* said. "It says in Matthew 5:4 that 'Blessed are those who mourn; they will be comforted.' While you're grieving, pray and God will give you the strength to help you get through each day."

He took her hand in his rough, calloused one. "Let's pray together now as a family for you, Beth, Henry, and for your sweet baby."

She cleared her throat and said, "Pray, too, that my labor will start soon so I won't have to have it induced." Beth didn't want to wait around for days to have her infant. She wanted to see her daughter soon.

And while holding her, she'd tell how much they loved her and how someday they would see her in heaven.

Chapter Thirteen

After leaving the Kings' residence, Chloe wished she could talk to someone about what had happened. It was unbelievable that Beth's baby was dead. She couldn't wrap her head around that this had occurred to her Amish friend. It was so heart-wrenching. What could have caused the baby to die?

Chloe thought how her parents enjoyed hearing about her friendship with Beth. They'd asked her several questions about the Amish, and thought it was nice she'd learned a lot about their way of life. Always being the doctor, her mother had asked if there were any birth defects in their community. Chloe thought that was an unusual question, but then her mom mentioned she'd read there were several Amish families with special needs children in Ohio. Chloe replied she hadn't heard of any, and Beth had never mentioned it being something occurring in their community.

When Chloe told them how Violet Robinson planned to join the Amish church, her dad said he bet that seldom happened for a woman with Violet's background.

Although she never could be Amish, Chloe could see many advantages to it. She loved how close Beth was to her family. It was their closeness she envied. Even though Beth had complained about her bishop father not wanting his daughters to work in Fields Corner, she'd mentioned recently that he might allow Priscilla to work in the fabric store. Apparently, Lillian King thought it would be good for Priscilla to work part-time in the store, and like many Amish husbands, he did respect his wife's viewpoint. Beth said maybe her working in the florist's shop had helped pave the way for her father to change his mind.

Chloe wondered if Violet becoming part of the King family had also made a difference. Having this close connection to a non-Amish woman might have made him decide to become more lenient about allowing his daughters to work among other Englishers in Fields Corner. Everyone loved Violet, especially Luke King. Smiling, Chloe thought how sweet it was that God had brought two worlds together through the romance of Luke and Violet.

She'd never acted on Beth's suggestion to talk to Violet about adoption, because later it hadn't seemed necessary. After talking with Karen and Jeff on Saturday, she felt like they might make the best parents for her baby girl. In fact, she'd called them on yesterday to tell Karen that she was almost positive if she put her baby up for adoption, she wanted them to be the parents. The word *almost* was important, because a small part of her still wanted to keep her daughter.

Remembering Karen's reaction stirred up different emotions for her: one was of happiness that she was giving her daughter to a couple not able to get pregnant, but at the same time she felt a deep loss that adoption meant she'd be without her baby.

After Karen had thanked her several times, she'd said, "I already have a lot of the baby items. I have the crib, rocking chair, monitor, diapers, diaper bag, bottles, fitted crib sheets, car seat, toys, and tons of adorable onesies. I have the drawers organized so when a midnight changing is necessary, I'll be able to find immediately what I need for our baby."

"Sounds like you thought of everything."

"We were expecting to adopt another baby several months ago, but the mother changed her mind and kept her baby."

Before her phone call to Karen, Chloe had asked her parents again if they might change their minds and support her in keeping the baby. Sadly, her mom said that it wasn't the best thing to do. Her mother even said how later Chloe would thank them for remaining strong in their decision. Her dad said he agreed with her mother, but wished things could be different. When she heard his resigned voice, she knew then there was no hope in changing her parents' minds.

Remembering Aunt Angie offering her a place to stay with her baby, she'd called Grandma Parrish to see if she could help raise her great-granddaughter. With two women's support, she could work part-time at the restaurant and maybe take a couple of online college classes, so her parents and siblings wouldn't view her as the loser in their family. It was a surprise to learn that Grandma was happily in love with an old college boyfriend. With both their spouses dead, they'd reconnected after years of being apart. That was why she hadn't returned to Fields Corner, and planned to stay the whole summer in Seattle. A wedding might be in the future for her grandmother.

Feeling restless and depressed, she thought about going for a walk. *I'll take my cell phone with me in case Beth needs me to drive her. I wish Tony wasn't working, because I'd text him to see if he wanted to join me. Maybe it's good he's at the office. I shouldn't bother him when he's been ignoring me.*

She wondered if Tony had been especially busy over the weekend. She'd been surprised she hadn't heard from him. Had Dr. Foster told him it wasn't a good idea to spend time with her outside the office, since she was a patient? She'd been relieved when her mom had denied knowing Dr. Cunningham. In fact, Chloe had felt ridiculous when she noticed how hurt her mother had been at her question. It'd been crazy to think in the first place that her mom had gotten Dr. Foster to hire the young and attractive Tony to keep tabs on her. Besides, he hadn't tried to influence her to put the baby up for adoption.

Her pregnancy had caused many changes. Her life had become something entirely different from what she had envisioned it would be this summer. It was really something that Tony and Beth had not been part of her life a few months ago, and now they were the ones she felt the closest to. Chloe seldom heard from her friend Megan. Although she understood Megan wasn't in the States, it was odd how they'd been friends for years, and now she no longer heard anything from her. If Megan had been the one to get pregnant, Chloe would have stayed in contact and tried to be there for her.

She had planned on telling Beth her adoption news, but then she'd called for a ride to the doctor's office. It hadn't seemed like a good time to talk about her baby. Then when she'd heard the shocking news about Beth's baby dying, Chloe definitely hadn't wanted to tell her how she'd decided on Karen and Jeff to adopt her baby, and had already notified them of her decision.

How awful life had become—giving her baby away would be a loss she'd feel for the rest of her life, but Chloe was positive Beth would also feel an incredible loss. For a child to die had to be the worst thing for a mother to endure.

Could their grieving for their losses create an even closer friendship that might last past the summer? Or would they go their separate paths, not wanting to be reminded of what hopes and dreams had died for both of them?

* * *

Late afternoon, Beth's father drove them home. Once the buggy stopped in front of their white farmhouse, he pulled her to him. She buried her head in his chest. Feeling his beating heart gave her the comfort and security she required. His father's love eased her pain for a moment. What was it about your parents that when you were at rock bottom, they somehow managed to give you the strength to face tragedy? Beth wondered. Their never-ending love was always there for you to tap into, so you could survive a terrible loss.

But could her heart survive losing her baby?

"I love you, Daddy," Beth murmured, as she remained in the circle of his comforting arms.

"I love you too." He loosened his hold of her and stared into her eyes. "Call anytime you want. We'll be here for you whenever you need anything."

"*Danki*," she said, noticing Henry was already on the ground, waiting to help her down.

After Henry assisted her out of the buggy, she said, "I'm going to gather the eggs. I never did it today."

"I can get the eggs. Why don't you go in the house and rest?"

"I want to do something that I usually do. I need a bit of a routine." Beth walked to the porch and picked up the egg basket. She had to hurry and get into the chicken coop before she broke down and cried again. Wanting to be alone for a bit was another reason she needed to escape.

Henry removed his straw hat and tossed it on a metal chair. "Okay, I'll go to the barn and take care of the livestock."

Entering the chicken coop, she took a deep breath. Going to each nest to get the eggs suddenly was overwhelming and too difficult. A rush of anger went through her body at the unfairness of losing her daughter. She wanted to scream in pain and yell at God for allowing this tragedy in her life and Henry's. *I can't scream. It'll frighten Henry and he'll come running to see if I'm hurt.*

A strong sense of bitterness rose inside her. She held an egg in her hand for a second, and then aimed it at the wall. She let the egg fly and it spattered against the wood. Because of the intensity of her many emotions, Beth had a deep feeling of loneliness, and she knew why. Without the active and strong kicking of her child, she felt deprived.

The only way she could cope was to have her baby today. Waiting for several days would not be the best for anyone. Having labor induced frightened her, but hoping for contractions to start soon was not an option for her. Yearning to hold their baby in her arms was what she needed to do instead of continuing to carry her dead child inside her womb.

In a rush, she gathered the remaining eggs and left the chicken coop to go to the barn to tell Henry what she wanted to do.

* * *

When Chloe heard her ringtone, she quickly left the kitchen to go to the living room to answer it. Maybe Tony had decided to call her. She looked down at the coffee table where her phone was, and the caller was Beth.

Quickly, she answered, knowing that her friend needed her.

"Chloe, I want to have my baby today. It feels so awful to have her dead inside me. I want to see her and tell her how much I love her and always will."

"That's good you decided to do this instead of waiting for your labor to start. I'm glad you called me."

"I called Violet and she said to go to the hospital. She's going to call Dr. Cunningham, and Violet promised to be there for me. Could you pick me and Henry up and drive us to the hospital? I'm sorry to bother you again, but a driver we've used in the past isn't available."

"I'll leave right now." Chloe hesitated, wondering if she should offer to pick up Beth's parents. She imagined that Beth would want her mom and dad at the hospital for support. Maybe she felt like it was asking too much of her to pick up them too. "I can take you first to the hospital and then I'll go get your parents."

"You don't have to get them. I left a message on their answering machine and told them I decided to have my labor induced. Henry left a message for his parents too. We wanted them to know but told them it's okay for them not to come to the hospital."

Violet thought it was a shame the King family didn't have a phone in their house, so Beth could talk to her mom before leaving. "Make sure you pack a bag in case you have to spend the night."

"Violet mentioned that too. She also told me to bring clothes for the baby that I had planned for her to wear home. She's never experienced a stillbirth as a midwife, but another nurse said parents find it helpful to make memories of the time spent with your child. And to take your time looking at, touching, and talking to your baby, because this is a memory that will last a lifetime. Violet said she'll make sure we get an imprint of handprints and footprints. She said some parents like to take pictures of their baby, but she knows that might be something I don't feel comfortable doing."

"That's good Violet could give you ways to make memories with your baby. Is there anything I can do for you?" Chloe wanted to do something positive for Beth, but couldn't think of anything that might help her.

"There is something I'd like you to do. Could you take a picture of our baby with your smartphone? I'd ask Violet, but she is going to be busy with taking care of the whole birthing process." Beth paused for a moment. "And I don't feel comfortable asking her because she's started her instructions to join our church. We don't believe in taking pictures, but I decided in this situation it should be okay."

"I'll take a picture. It might be nice to have one of you holding your daughter. I can take it without your face showing." Chloe knew some Amish used pictures of their children in ads for their cottage businesses. She was amazed that Beth could even function and knew what she wanted to do after the birth. *It's good that Violet could give her positive things to focus on,* Chloe thought.

"Chloe, I know this is a lot to ask you to do for me, so maybe you can go home to sleep for a few hours."

"No, it's not a problem. I'll stay in the waiting room, and whenever you want me to take pictures, I will. Or anything you need, don't hesitate to tell me. Thank you for including me. It means a lot to me to share this special time with you."

Chapter Fourteen

A little after eight o'clock on Monday evening, Beth had her baby girl. While Violet cleaned up the baby, tears streamed down Beth's face. Through his own tears, Henry said gently, "Beth, you're the bravest woman I know. It was *gut* you had your labor induced. Our baby girl is beautiful."

"Henry's right. She's beautiful," Violet said, in a choked voice.

Her husband's attempt at trying to comfort her meant a lot. "I couldn't bear to continue carrying her. It didn't seem right. I can't believe how healthy and fully developed she looks. I wish we knew what caused her death."

Jennifer, a nurse with brown hair and freckles, stood next to Beth's side. "She probably hasn't been gone that long, because her coloring is one of the best I've seen in a stillborn."

As she held the lifeless baby close to her chest, Violet said, "I wrapped her in a receiving blanket for now. I thought you might like to sometime put her in the white dress your mother made."

"I was surprised when she crocheted a dress. It was like she knew we'd have a baby girl."

Violet placed the infant in Beth's arms. "She weighs six pounds and five ounces. Her length is eighteen inches."

"Did you decide on a name?" Jennifer asked.

"Henry and I decided on Nora Marie."

"Nora Marie Byler is a wonderful name and perfect for such a lovely girl," Violet said, looking at the newborn.

"Violet or Jennifer, could you tell Chloe to come in? I'll have her take pictures of Nora before my family and Henry's come in. Just explain that I thought Chloe might want to get home soon."

Jennifer touched her shoulder briefly. "We do have a professional photographer who will take pictures of your daughter, you, and your family for free. He's done this in the past for stillborns."

Beth shook her head. "*Danki*, but that will be too much to do. If Chloe gets a few pictures, that will be fine. Amish don't believe in taking pictures, but I think an exception in this case can be made for a few photos."

"I'll go get Chloe. I'll tell your family that Chloe needs to go home and rest so they won't take it personally she gets to see Nora first." Violet gave Beth a concerned look. "Don't forget to drink your apple juice."

"I will, and *danki*, Violet." Beth swallowed hard, knowing how painful this death had been on all of them in the room. "I'm glad you and Jennifer have been here with us. You have made this experience more bearable and have been awesome."

Violet and Jennifer both cried when she'd pushed her baby into the world that she would never see or experience. Both women answered questions she'd had during the induced labor. And Dr. Cunningham had been great with making frequent trips to check her progress. His overwhelming kindness made her realize that her original disappointment at having him this morning instead of Dr. Foster had been wrong.

After Violet left to fetch Chloe, Beth stared at her baby and said, "I love you. Your daddy and I will always love you, Nora Marie. You will never be forgotten." *Henry should get to hold her before Chloe comes into the room to take pictures.* Beth gave Henry their baby and said, "Daddy, here's your daughter to hold."

Tears pricked Henry's eyes as he gazed at Nora. "She has your dark brown hair."

Their baby looked tiny in Henry's big muscled arms. Looking at her daughter and husband, Beth realized with her whole soul that things should have been so different. Even though it had been painful, she had no regrets having her baby. She was like a little angel.

"*Ya*. She reminds me of Sadie when she was a baby. I was ten years old when Sadie was born. She has the same nose and same amount of dark hair. Later Sadie's baby hair fell out and it came in auburn. I wonder if Nora's hair would have been a different color later."

"Would you like to sit in the rocking chair for a picture?" Jennifer motioned toward the oak chair in the room. "I think that might be nice."

Beth nodded, noticing a yellow and green afghan thrown over the chair. "That's a great idea. I'll dress her first before I move to the chair." Glancing at Henry, she said, "You keep holding her. I don't want us to rush this time with her."

"It's hard having this happen"—Henry took his eyes off Nora for a second to look at Beth—"but the spirit is very strong in this room. Seeing Nora gives me a sense of peace, and I feel our heavenly Father's love."

"I feel His love too. I have unanswerable questions running through my mind, but I'm trying to keep focusing on the little bit of time we have with our daughter. I feel like she's here with us in spirit."

A few minutes later, Beth put the white dress on Nora, but did it while Henry continued holding her. When she felt Nora's cold little feet, Beth said to Henry, "It's hard to realize that I can't warm her up. Her feet are so cold." Next, she carefully put white booties on Nora's feet.

Violet brought Chloe with her when returning to the hospital room. She immediately went to see the baby.

"Nora is beautiful." Chloe tenderly touched the baby's small hand. "She has such a look of peace on her face."

"I told everyone what you named her and told them what she weighs." Violet smiled. "They are all anxious to see her, so maybe Chloe better take the pictures soon. I don't see them waiting patiently much longer. There's a lot of love in the waiting room, and both families want to share it now with you, Beth, Henry, and little Nora."

Beth moved to the rocking chair. Chloe dropped her handbag on the end of the bed. "Is it okay if I hold her before I take the pictures?"

Standing, Chloe took Nora from Henry at his nod and Beth's verbal yes. Chloe caressed Nora so gently. "She has long eyelashes. Nora looks like a sleeping angel with a smile on her perfect face." Chloe's blue eyes filled with tears. "She's so precious."

* * *

Two days later, the Byler and King families had the funeral for Nora Marie. Violet's tears would not stop as she and Luke left the cemetery. Holding Violet's hand tightly in his, Luke wished there was something he could say to comfort her. But the truth was that he was grieving, too, that his baby niece had been born dead. Remembering how happy Beth had been all during her pregnancy, it broke his heart to see the baby in a small pine box. It was unreal that this had happened to their family.

Out of the corner of his eye, Luke saw Chloe hugging Beth. "It's nice Chloe came to the cemetery too. Beth and she became good *freinden* in such a short time."

"They seemed to bond instantly because of their youth . . . and their pregnancies." In the midst of her tears, Violet gave him a tiny smile. "Once again two people have found much in common even though they're from different worlds. I hope they can stay in touch when Chloe goes back to Cincinnati to live, but maybe that won't be possible."

"Maybe she'll stay in Fields Corner."

"I think Dr. Cunningham might like that."

Violet had mentioned to him that Dr. Cunningham was going to stay in Fields Corner for two years and work with Dr. Foster, but hearing about the young doctor being interested in Chloe surprised Luke. It was also a relief, because Tony Cunningham working closely with his lovely Violet had worried him a little. Well, maybe it worried him more than a little. He was a young, handsome doctor, and English. Someone Violet should want to marry instead of an Amish man with a buggy store. Violet spent a lot of time at the doctor's office and the birthing center, so he hoped Chloe stayed in the area. "That's good to hear. I haven't been thrilled about you working with a single English man."

"You don't have to worry about me with anyone else." She squeezed his hand. "I'm in love with you. Anyhow, I might not be working much longer as a midwife."

"I don't understand. You love being a midwife." Being one to the Amish mothers was one of the reasons he felt she could fit easier into the Plain world.

"I need to talk to you, but not here." Violet glanced at his black buggy. "We can't stay and talk in your buggy because everyone walking by us will wonder why we aren't leaving right away to go to your parents' for the meal."

The sadness in her eyes caught him like a physical blow, and he knew it was serious what she wanted to tell him. Apparently, Violet didn't want to talk while he drove the buggy. If she needed his full and undivided attention, it had to be extremely important. "We can take the long way to my parents' and stop at the town's park."

He helped her into his buggy, and then walked around to the hitching post to untie his horse.

Within ten minutes, they were sitting on a park bench facing a pond surrounded by trees and flowers in pinks, reds, and purples. A few men and children fished on the opposite side of the water.

A fleeting look of sorrow crossed Violet's face. "Such a beautiful summer day and we are dressed in black for a baby's death. Babies aren't supposed to die. One thing I love about being a midwife is experiencing the miracle of life each time, but when Nora was born dead, I felt a sense of failure and loss. My purpose is to help a mother achieve a successful pregnancy with a healthy baby at the end of the nine months."

"Violet, you have done that over and over again. You're a *wunderbaar* midwife. Look how you delivered Molly's baby on the side of the road before you even had any training. I don't think my sister will ever forget what you did." Molly hadn't expected to have a quick labor with her firstborn. It would have been more frightening if Violet hadn't taken charge and been calm.

"It was awful holding Nora and wanting to do what I usually do. From instinct, I reached for my suction when she was in Dr. Cunningham's hands, but I pulled my hand back when I realized I didn't need to do that. Even though I was riveted by the look of peace of Nora's face, I wanted to scream at God for taking this baby's life." Violet's lower lip quivered. "I missed seeing Nora's little fist grabbing at life. I wanted to massage life into her body, but I wasn't needed to do anything. Death had already taken her."

It *had* occurred to him how hard it must have been for Violet to witness Nora's sad entry into the world, but not so much that she'd want to quit being a midwife. What should have been a joyous event had turned into a heartbreaking one. "You're right. Babies are the least expected to die, so when it happens it's a shock to everyone. But you can't quit being a midwife because of Nora's death."

She frowned at him. "What if this is a sign from God that I should quit being a midwife? If it had happened much later in my career, it would be different, but for it to occur now and especially to your sister makes me question everything. Maybe I missed something during her last prenatal visit."

"I'm sure you didn't miss anything. No one knows what caused Nora's death. It wasn't anyone's fault. Not yours, not the doctors or Beth's." Luke searched his memory for Scripture to recite that might give Violet comfort. When a couple of his favorite verses came to his mind, he said, "Maybe these words of our Lord from Peter will help you. 'Humble yourselves, therefore, under God's mighty hand, that he may lift you up in due time. Cast all your anxiety on him because he cares for you.' Quitting as a midwife won't bring Nora back, but doing what you do best is a gift from God. You are almost finished with your college work and will be a certified nurse-midwife. God has blessed you."

Violet leaned her head against his shoulder. "He certainly blessed me when I met you."

Chapter Fifteen

It should have been a great July day playing in the sand with Tyler before lunchtime, but it wasn't, Chloe thought. Although it was a gorgeous day with lots of sunshine and summer breezes, her heart felt heavy. She couldn't stop worrying about Beth and Henry. She'd taken three meals to them because even though Beth didn't have a baby to take care of, it was still important for her to physically take it easy.

Each time she'd gone to visit, Lillian King had been there. In private, Beth's mother mentioned how worried they were about her. It'd been four weeks since the funeral, and Lillian said it'd been hard to get Beth out of bed each day. Her daughter had lost interest in everything. Even though Beth didn't care about getting out of bed, Chloe could tell from her friend's drooping shoulders and dull-looking eyes that she hadn't had much sleep.

While putting grilled cheese sandwiches on plates, Chloe wondered how long it'd take Beth to take part in life again. Surely, in time, Beth would recover from this shock. Chloe knew Beth would never forget Nora, but hoped her friend could enjoy life again. When her cell phone rang, Chloe looked at it and saw Karen was calling. Since their meeting at Outback Steakhouse, Karen had called her several times. "Tyler, I'm going to take this call."

"Don't talk too long. Your sandwich will get cold," Tyler said.

Tyler is such a cute little kid. Chloe grinned at her blond-haired cousin. "I was thinking if I took too long on the phone, you'd probably eat mine."

He grinned back at her. "I won't."

Pressing the phone against her ear, Chloe said, "Hello, Karen."

"Hi, Chloe. I'm glad I reached you. I didn't wake you up from a nap, did I?"

"No. I'm taking care of my cousin today while his mom's at work."

"I feel guilty that I haven't paid for any of your medical expenses. I talked with your mom but she insists I don't need to. Is there anything I can do for you to make things easier for you?"

Even though she'd told Karen that she'd chosen them to be parents for her baby, she had made it clear that she might still change her mind. Maybe Logan would have a change of heart and want to see their daughter. He could fall in love with their baby and want to be a father.

"That's sweet of you, Karen, but I can't think of anything I need."

"You don't sound like yourself. Are you feeling okay?" Karen asked.

Should she mention the death of Beth's infant? *I don't want to increase Karen's anxiety that something might happen to my baby. It has to be hard to be in her situation, waiting for years to become a mother. Well, I might as well be truthful and explain why I'm feeling sad.* "I'm worried about my friend Beth. She lost her baby. She only had a month left when the baby stopped moving. I'm sure it's going to take time for Beth to get over what happened."

"I'm so sorry to hear that. That's awful news. Does she have other children?"

"No, it was their first baby."

"Does Beth live in Fields Corner? Or is she your friend from Cincinnati?"

"Beth and her husband grew up here. I met her at the doctor's office, and we hit it off immediately."

"I'm sure having you for a friend plus her family will give her the support she needs during this sad time."

"I hope so."

"I just had a thought. I've heard a lot of Amish live in Fields Corner. My sister, Jane, and I could visit you and go to some Amish stores. Jane loves anything Amish. Personally, I don't understand why the Amish want to live the way they do. It seems weird to me. I don't get why they believe it's wrong to use electricity and they only drive buggies. Jane thinks it's charming they have buggies for their transportation, but it's too unsafe for their children. I read recently how several young children died in a buggy accident."

Hearing the judgmental tone in Karen's voice upset Chloe. She needed to defend her friend's beliefs. In a sharp voice, she said, "Beth is Amish. The Plain people live simple lives because God and family are important to them. They believe it's important to live separate from the world. The Amish think if electricity exists in a home, the TV will be turned on while another person might go use a computer and get on the Internet. The family will be split and not as close. They also feel owning cars cause families to go in too many different directions instead of remaining a strong Christian unit."

Karen cleared her throat. "Thanks for explaining why the Amish choose to live without electricity and cars. That's special you have an Amish friend. I imagine it's been great learning more about their culture."

"It has been." Feeling emotional and close to tears, Chloe wanted to end the conversation. Maybe it was her pregnancy hormones, but she found Karen's attitude offensive. Was Karen always critical of people with different values? "I'm taking care of Tyler today, so I better get off here."

* * *

Two weeks later, on a Saturday night, Chloe decided to call Logan. Angie and Tyler had gone to the store, so she got comfortable on the loveseat in the living room. Looking down at her baby bump, she thought how Logan hadn't even seen her in person for weeks. She'd texted him a picture of herself last week to jog his memory of her. She had worn an adorable pink top with her jean capris. He'd only texted back how she looked cute.

The European vacation had ended a few days ago, so that meant Logan was back home in Indian Hill. She had expected her boyfriend to visit her, but he'd started working for his dad immediately to earn extra money for college. She had offered to go home to see him, but he said that it wasn't a good time for him.

It was disappointing that he couldn't come see her in Fields Corner. She missed him so much, and wanted him to see the picturesque small town.

When he answered her call, Chloe said, "Logan, I miss you. I need to see you soon. Our baby's due next month. We should get together before she's born."

"I'm sorry I haven't made a trip to see you. I know you want us to be together to raise the baby, but that's not going to happen. We are too young to be parents. I'm glad you chose parents to adopt her. You told me they have wanted a child for a long time. The baby will be a blessing for them."

Something else was wrong. His voice sounded funny, but she wasn't brave enough to ask what was bothering him. "I might not give our baby to Karen and Jeff. I'm having second thoughts about them."

"Well, it's up to you. I'm sure in the end you will choose the right parents." There was a definite sharpness to his voice now. "Chloe, there's something I should tell you. I was going to wait, but that's not fair to you."

Surely Logan's not going to break up with me. He told me he loved me. After a moment of complete silence, she said, "I love you, Logan."

"Chloe, don't make it harder than it already is. Megan and I are a couple. We didn't mean for it to happen, but we got close in Europe. I'm sorry."

No wonder I never heard from Megan all summer. She was busy stealing my boyfriend from me. "You never should have gone to Europe. You had a responsibility to stay with me . . . the mother of your baby. Is it because I got pregnant that you're dumping me for Megan?"

Chloe heard Logan exhaling a deep breath while she waited for him to respond. When he didn't, she said bitterly, "I can't believe you are dating Megan. How could you do this to me?"

"Chloe, I didn't mean for it to happen, but after spending time together in Europe, we realized we were in love. I didn't mean to hurt you. That's another reason I don't want you to keep the baby. I'll feel like I have to also be part of the baby's life. It'd be too awkward when we are no longer together."

Tears blurred her vision, and she rapidly blinked them away. "I'm sorry you are the father of my baby. She deserved better."

"Then you should definitely not have a problem giving her to loving adoptive parents. I need to go. I hope everything goes well for you. Bye, Chloe."

Slumping against the back of the small sofa, Chloe realized how truly alone she was. She had so much hurt inside of her from what Logan had said to her. Some of the pain came from him breaking up with her, but even more pain was in her heart because he thought so little of her and their baby. He could have done the right thing and married her. But no, he'd chosen to be with her best friend.

Obviously I have to give up my ridiculous hope of being a family with my baby. Chloe put her hand on her belly, savoring her child's forceful movements. "I want you to have a wonderful family life where you're a priority and not an afterthought," she whispered. "Your grandparents think I'm too young to keep you. I can't count on my grandma. She's busy reconnecting with an old love."

Although Aunt Angie had offered to help if she kept the baby, that didn't seem like the best option for her child. She wanted her daughter to have both a father and a mother.

What should I do? Making this colossal decision is overwhelming. I need to pray for help.

Bowing her head, she prayed, "Dear Lord, please guide me in making the best decision in choosing adoptive parents for my precious unborn child. I want her to grow up in a loving Christian home. I love her so much and want what is the best for her." Tears streamed down her face, and she paused for a minute. "I'm not sure now about Karen and Jeff, but I hate to rule them out completely. She seemed too judgmental about Amish people, and that worries me. And help me to get past the hurt I feel from Logan not loving me any longer. Thank you for forgiving me for my sins and for your great love. In Jesus' name, I pray."

A verse that had helped her in the past was one she needed now—*I can do all things through Christ which strengtheneth me.*

Depending on divine guidance would give her the answer that she needed in choosing the best parents, but what about the void in her heart that only a true love could fill? Deep down she had suspected that Logan wasn't going to be her true love, but she hadn't wanted to face the truth. Now she had no choice, and had to accept that she'd lost Logan to Megan.

Maybe God had someone else for her that would truly love her forever.

Chapter Sixteen

"*Danki*, Beth, for breakfast. It was *appeditlich*."

Looking at her broad-shouldered husband, Beth felt guilt that she hadn't fixed Henry's breakfast for a long time. Too many sleepless nights had caused her to lack the energy to do anything about getting up early to cook breakfast. Henry hadn't complained. Holding her *kaffi* cup in her hands, she murmured, "I'm trying to do better, but it's hard. I feel broken inside."

"I'm grieving too. We need to heal together. You've been shutting me out."

Henry's serious face, pain flickering in his eyes, made her uncomfortable. She knew her continued depression worried him. Many times she had wanted to voice her fears to him but couldn't. Instead, the fears festered inside her. Although he grieved deeply Nora's death, he was able to do his farm work, while she couldn't do housework. Daily routine tasks took too much effort for her. Twisting a lock of hair around her finger, she said, "I can't stop feeling responsible. Maybe I did something wrong while I was pregnant. Maybe God thought I wasn't ready to be a mother."

"I'm sure that isn't true. And you were already an excellent mother to Nora. You did everything right during your pregnancy. It wasn't your fault that she died." He hesitated, gauging her for a moment. "I want you to talk to me about your feelings. Don't hold back. I love you, Beth. We also have our whole community praying for us. Don't close yourself off to people."

She knew why he said that. When people visited her, it was easier to say little and hope they'd leave her alone. "I can't help it. None of them knows what it's like losing a baby after carrying her for months in my womb. When Caroline and Naomi came to see me, it was uncomfortable for all of us." They had been her closest friends, but there were many things she couldn't begin to share with them. Life and death had changed her.

"If you want to talk to another mother about having a stillborn, I can get you a cell phone so you can. I already talked to your father, and he said that's fine."

She knew Violet had suggested they go to a support group for parents who had experienced the death of a baby. Violet said she could share her feelings and Nora's story. But she didn't want to go to a group like that. What good would it do? It wouldn't bring Nora back. Talking with someone about it on a cell phone wasn't something she wanted to do either, but it was thoughtful of Henry to make the suggestion.

"I'll think about it," she murmured.

"Is there anything I can get you before I go to do the chores? I noticed you haven't eaten anything."

Putting her cup down, she shook her head. "*Danki*, but I'll eat something later." She decided to share the awful thoughts she had about Chloe with Henry. "You know, what also hurts me a lot is Chloe being pregnant. I don't want her baby to die like Nora did, but I don't understand why we lost Nora, and Chloe doesn't seem to know what to do about her daughter. It's not fair."

She gulped hard, trying not to sob. Henry stood and walked to her. Wrapping his arm around her shoulder and kissing her tenderly on the cheek, he said gently, "It doesn't seem fair, but we have to have faith."

"I feel like I lost my faith when Nora died."

"Remember how the disciples and Jesus were in their ship in the midst of a storm. They became afraid and wondered why Jesus hadn't done anything. They found he was asleep, and once he woke up, Jesus calmed the winds. He said to them, 'I am with you always, even unto the end of the world.' We are experiencing a storm in our lives now. I can tell you have lost your energy to go on, and each day is hard for you. Maybe that verse from Matthew will help you when you feel like life is too much to deal with."

After Henry left to do the morning chores, Beth thought about Chloe. Glancing at the calendar on the wall, she realized Henry had flipped the page to August. *Chloe's due date is this month.* Maybe she should give her some of the baby items she had ready for their child, but, of course, not if Chloe wasn't keeping her. But how could she give her baby away? It was just too hard to comprehend that a mother could give her child to strangers. But with people not able to have children, it was blessing for them to be able to adopt.

I would know what Chloe's plans are if I hadn't cut her out of my life too. I even avoided returning her phone calls. She called and left messages on the answering machine to see how I was. Several times she dropped food off so I wouldn't have to cook.

But the truth was it hurt too much to see Chloe pregnant and remember how quickly their friendship had grown because of their expanding bellies. Chloe had been there for her when she needed a ride to see Dr. Cunningham, and again to go to the hospital. She'd never hesitated or said no to her requests. And she'd appreciated the several photos of Nora that Chloe had taken in the hospital and printed for her. Nora's little face looked peaceful and beautiful to her.

Walking to the sink, she turned on the water and rinsed her cup. The sun shone brightly through the window. While she looked at the outside view of the red barn and yard, Beth said out loud, "Why, God? Why did you take Nora?"

* * *

"Thank you for having me over to eat," Chloe said, sitting next to a small patio table. Tony sat across from her, looking so hot to her. It was hard to keep her eyes off his well-proportioned, muscular body. His gray T-shirt fitted snugly on his body, so that didn't help any, but fortunately, she was hungry, so had to take time to cut her meat and slather more sour cream on her potato. It wouldn't do to keep staring at her doctor. *What would I have done if I hadn't met Tony?* He'd been a lifesaver to her this summer with Logan missing from her life.

"I'm glad now I bought this house. I wasn't sure about buying it, since I might only stay two years in Fields Corner, but I didn't feel like renting an apartment. I like having my own yard, and this street is quiet."

"I don't blame you. You got your house for a great price with the owners anxious to move." She grinned. "You might even change your mind about home births and decide to stay longer."

"That's what Paul is hoping." His eyes widened as he stared at her. "Hey, would you feel like going furniture shopping with me sometime? I bought my bedroom furniture from Samuel Weaver, and my parents gave me a sofa they didn't want any longer, but I need to get a table and chairs for the kitchen."

"I'd love to, but we'll have to go soon. I only have a month left."

He frowned. "That's true. You don't have much longer. Maybe it isn't a good idea."

"I want to go. I need something to take my mind off everything. I'm anxious to see my baby, but at the same time I'm not looking forward to labor."

"I hope you have a short labor. With all your walking, maybe that exercise will help."

"I wonder if the ice cream cones we get during our walks cancel the benefits of walking."

His brown eyes twinkled. "I'm sure they don't. Calcium's important for the baby."

"I knew there was a reason I like you as my doctor." Chloe stopped eating her meat and potato to pick up her ear of corn. She loved the delicious corn. "How did you get the corn to turn out so perfect? It's moist."

"I put an ice cube with each ear of corn when I wrapped them in foil."

"I never would've thought of doing that. I'll have to tell my dad to put ice cubes with his corn when he grills."

Tony glanced at the two clay pots with red and white petunias on his deck. "Thanks for the flowers. My mom commented on how pretty they are."

"You're welcome."

"When my parents came to visit last weekend, they were disappointed you weren't here."

During their last month's visit, she had met Tony's parents and liked them a lot. "I'm sorry I missed them. I went home to see my family and tried talking again with my parents about keeping my baby."

"How did that go?"

"Not well. My parents, especially my mom, want me to get a college degree. That's one of the reasons she doesn't want me to keep my baby. She's afraid I won't go to college if I have a baby to take care of, but I know I could go to college part-time and still keep my baby."

"I think you could too."

She swallowed a bite of potato and felt happy that Tony believed in her. But it didn't surprise her. He'd been supportive and great to her all summer. When Logan had broken her heart, she'd cried on Tony's chest. "Thanks. I don't know what I would have done without you this summer. If I hadn't been pregnant, I never would've met you. It's great how you decided to take this job in a small town. Most doctors aren't willing to take on a job working in an Amish community."

"I'll admit I wasn't sure at first, but I like the small-town atmosphere here." He took a deep breath. "Is your plan to go home after you give birth?"

She shrugged. "I guess. It's funny how in the beginning I hated leaving my home to come here to live this summer, but now I know I'll miss Fields Corner. And I've been praying all the time about what to do about my baby. I feel God is also telling me to go the adoption path. I think that's why I haven't thought of any names for her. I know that should be something that the adoptive parents decide. I hate that I'm not keeping her, but I have to think what is best for my daughter. I want her to have a mother and a father."

"I'm sorry. You haven't had it easy."

Chloe noticed that he didn't say he agreed with her that it was better to have two parents. *Well, that's probably because he knows it is too.* She sipped her iced tea. "I'm going to at least hold and love her for a couple of days."

"I'm glad you are." Tony put his silverware on his plate. "Would it be okay if I visit you sometime? We could go to a Bengals game."

"I'd like that a lot." She grinned. "We should go when the Bengals play the Browns. I know the Bengals will beat your team."

He chuckled. "Hey, I don't think so."

"Are you ready to try my cheesecake?" She had remembered his mother mentioning how much her son liked cheesecake, so she'd offered to provide the dessert for the evening. Her nanny, Kelly, always made a yummy cheesecake, so she used her recipe.

"I am definitely anxious to eat it. Let's go inside. It's pretty hot out here."

She stood and said, "It does seem hotter now."

He held the door open for her to enter the kitchen first. After they both placed their plates on the kitchen counter, Tony pulled her into his arms. "I'm going to miss you."

She looked into his eyes and felt her heart race. "I'm going to miss you too."

He gently pressed his lips to her cheek. "I've wanted to kiss you ever since the first walk we took together."

"Why didn't you?" she asked in a teasing tone.

"I was afraid I'd scare you away."

"That would never happen."

"What about our age difference?"

"I like that you're older. You aren't an immature boy, but a wonderful and amazing man." She reached out and traced lightly along his face. "My last year of high school was supposed to be perfect, but as soon as I realized I was pregnant, things began falling apart. First, my trip to Europe was canceled. Then I was told I needed to leave my home to live with my aunt. I was crushed, but now I'm glad everything happened the way it did. You've become important to me."

"You mean a lot to me too." As his lips covered hers, she felt fluttery inside. His continued deep kisses stirred her senses. After several moments of kissing, her baby's strong movements startled her. "My daughter seems to want to get into the action."

Tony laughed. "I noticed."

As he continued holding her close, she said, "If I hadn't gotten pregnant, I might never have met you. God blessed me by bringing you into my life." What would the summer have been like if Tony had been absent from her life? She'd enjoyed being with him, and wondered if they could maintain a long-distance relationship.

"I almost didn't come to Fields Corner. I thought about taking a position at a hospital in Cleveland, but I kept feeling God wanted me to go elsewhere."

"I'm glad you followed God's urging and came to Fields Corner. You've given me so much support . . . and it's been fun spending time with you." Oh, how could she leave this small town when Tony was living here? At her sudden, unexpected tears, Chloe tried to stop crying. What was wrong with her? She should be on cloud nine that Tony cared about her.

"Chloe, you're crying. What's wrong?"

"I don't know." She buried her face against his chest. "I started thinking about me not being here and being back at home."

"I don't want to stop seeing you. Cincinnati isn't that far away. I'll visit you so much that you might get tired of me."

Lifting her head, she said, "That will never happen. I will never get tired of being with you." At an especially sharp movement, Chloe giggled. "I think my baby gave me another strong kick because she wants some cheesecake."

* * *

After Tony and Chloe finished watching a DVD, they went to the Swift residence in her aunt's neighborhood. Loretta and her husband, Frank, were welcoming, and even told Tony that if he ever needed anything to give them a call. Chloe liked to think of the older couple as her surrogate grandparents. Her mother's parents had both passed away when she was a child, and her Grandpa Parrish had been dead for five years.

Aunt Angie and her ex-husband, Jim, were considering getting married again. His alcoholism had caused their marriage to fail, but now he'd been sober for several months. Aunt Angie and Tyler had gone camping with Jim. Chloe hoped they could work everything out, so that marriage might work for them the second time around. Aunt Angie had wanted her to stay with Violet Robinson for the weekend, so she wouldn't be alone in the house. When Loretta insisted she stay with them, Aunt Angie liked how she could stay in their small town and wouldn't have to drive to Carrie Robinson's farmhouse.

It had been such a lovely night, Chloe thought. Tony had kissed her several times during the movie, and when she walked him out to his car, he said, "Hopefully the little one will let you get some sleep tonight."

With her hand on her belly, she said, "That would be nice, but I don't know if I'll be able to sleep anyhow. I've—"

At the sound of his ringtone, he said, "I better get this. I'm on call tonight. Paul and his wife took their youngest son to a college orientation. Paul won't be back until Sunday."

She was going to tell Tony what she'd decided to do about her precious baby. The parents she'd definitely wanted for her child had to be contacted soon.

"Chloe, I need to go to the hospital. She had fairly short labors before, and with it being her third child, it won't be long before she delivers. I'll call you tomorrow."

She only had two weeks left before her due date, but with Tony's medical interruption, sharing her choice of parents would have to wait. *That's what I get for dating an obstetrician.* "I hope her labor does go quickly."

Chapter Seventeen

On Saturday morning, Chloe sat in her car and decided to call her mother before going to see Beth and Henry. The August day was already hot and humid, but she wouldn't have to sit long in the car. Her telephone conversations with her mom never were long. With the windows down, there was a bit of a breeze. As soon as she started the engine to drive to Beth's house, she would turn the air conditioning on in the car. While waiting for her mom to answer, Chloe knew what she was about to tell her would not go over well.

After several rings, her mom answered and said in a rush, "I'm glad you called. I have some big news. You aren't in labor, I hope."

"No, I'm not, but I hope I will be soon. I only have two weeks left. What's your big news?" Could her mom have had a change of heart and want her to keep the baby? Not likely, but a girl could always hope.

"NBC News is going to do a feature on my clinic and the high success rate we've had with our cancer patients. I'm thrilled that we are getting this exposure on the national news. I'm getting ready to go to the clinic now, so I can't talk too long."

"Congratulations, Mom. That's awesome news. When is it going to be on TV?"

"They didn't give me the exact date, but it will air later this month. They are coming on Tuesday to interview my staff and me. I'm sure you won't have the baby this week. You'll probably go late anyhow, with it being your first. I always went past my due dates."

"Mom, I called to tell you that I want to give the baby to Beth and Henry."

"That's nice, sweetheart. I have a call to take. It's the NBC number. Bye."

Stunned, Chloe stared at her smartphone for a moment. Did her mother realize she was talking about an Amish couple being her child's parents? She expected to get arguments about her decision. For one, she had already selected Karen and Jeff, so thought that might be enough reason for her mom to object to the change. The couple had impressed her mom greatly, and obviously, her granddaughter being raised in a Plain community would be a red flag for her mom.

I better call Dad. I don't want any conflict after I give my daughter to Beth. When her call went to voicemail, Chloe realized if her parents couldn't be bothered with her calls on a Saturday, she would not call them when she started labor. She was done reaching out to them. There was no point in calling her siblings either, because she had never been close to Andrea or Carter. At age thirty-two, Andrea had been trying to get pregnant, so wasn't happy her little sister had managed to do what she hadn't accomplished. Carter was engaged to a woman named Daphne, and she seemed high-maintenance. Still, it would be nice if her brother made an effort to connect with her.

Now she felt one hundred percent confident about what she planned on doing. In her heart, she knew that the right thing to do was give the baby to Beth and Henry. If she had any reservations about giving her baby away, they were gone now. Her parents didn't even have time to talk with her on a weekend. How could she have ever expected them to give her the financial support she would require in raising her daughter? She shouldn't be surprised, but it still hurt. It seemed they hadn't cared about her for a long time.

Tears flowed and stung her eyes. The pain of being rejected again ripped her heart to shreds. Sniffing, she pulled a tissue out of her bag and blew her nose. *Why am I so unlovable that my parents, siblings, and Logan don't want me in their lives? They seem to be happier without me around. I need to be strong and give my baby the best home possible.*

* * *

"When do you think Henry will be home?" Chloe asked, sitting across from Beth at the table.

Seeing how pretty Chloe looked in her jean capris and blue floral blouse, Beth wished her appearance was better. She had slipped on a faded brown dress and hadn't done much with her hair. Putting it in a bun and wearing a *kapp* hadn't been essential with staying home since Nora's funeral. She couldn't remember what day she last took a shower. Everything had been too much effort, except she had fixed Henry's breakfast the last couple of days. That was progress, and now she needed to pull herself together, because Chloe hadn't given up on her. Her English friend had been consistent in trying to reach her.

"Henry's helping his *daed* with his dairy business this morning. I thought he'd be back by now. *Danki* for bringing cookies. They are delicious." Beth thought it sweet Chloe had baked her favorite oatmeal raisin cookies. She hoped Chloe would tell the reason soon for her early morning visit.

"I wanted to talk to you both, but I'll go ahead and tell you why I'm here. Well, maybe it's better this way and you can fill Henry in when he gets home." Chloe took a deep breath. "I've told you about my childhood and how a nanny raised me. I used to hope I'd get cancer, so that I would get attention from my mom . . . the kind she gives her patients. She's a devoted physician and spends a lot of time at the clinic."

"I'm sorry." *No wonder Chloe yearned to have a home with her boyfriend*, Beth thought.

"I want my baby to have a father and a mother. I had hopes Logan would want our baby and me so we could be a family. That's not what he wants. He broke up with me and is seeing my former best friend, Megan."

It was hard to believe Logan could break up with his pregnant girlfriend, but it must be awful for Chloe to also have lost him to her best friend. Beth had never thought much of Logan in the first place, but didn't think she should mention this fact. "That's awful. I'm sorry he treated you so badly."

"Me too." Chloe paused for a moment. "Without any support from my parents or Logan, I have decided adoption will be the best choice. I want my daughter to have two parents who will be around while she's growing up and will give her love. I'd like you and Henry to be my child's mother and father. I know you two will be the best parents she could ever have."

Chloe's adoption suggestion stunned Beth. A flood of emotions churned inside her, but the biggest shock was that she wanted to be a mother to Chloe's baby. Something didn't seem logical to her. Why would Chloe want her baby to be raised Amish? "Chloe, I'm honored you want me to become a mother to your daughter, but are you sure you want her raised in an Amish home?"

Chloe nodded quickly. "You mentioned how Amish adopt English children, and I think that's great. I love how the Amish are so family-oriented and close-knit. I never had that feeling of closeness like you do with your parents. I would like to go to an Amish church service sometime just to have the experience."

Beth gave a nervous laugh. "You might change your mind about an Amish upbringing for your baby when you sit on an uncomfortable bench for three hours."

"I won't. And I'd love to hear your father preach."

"He sometimes doesn't give the sermon. Before each service, the deacon, ministers, and my *daed* decide who will preach. While we sing hymns from the Ausbund—that's a special hymnal we use—the deacon, ministers, and bishop go to a room and decide who will be preaching the two sermons for that day."

"That's interesting."

I better bring up education to Chloe, because that is something her family might want for their granddaughter. Even though they want her to be adopted, I'm sure they expected Chloe to choose an English couple. "Aren't you worried that your daughter will only have an eighth-grade education? You graduated from high school and your parents want you to go to college."

Shaking her head, Chloe frowned. "I've seen firsthand what happens when you have a lot of education. I'll go to college, but I'm not sure if I'll graduate. My parents thrive on working all the time and they make a lot of money, but they don't have time to enjoy it. I don't want to end up like them."

"Well, we work hard, but as a family. Children start doing chores at a young age. One early thing they learn to do is to take care of the chickens and gather the eggs."

"I started doing chores when I was young too. My nanny had me do several things each day." Chloe grinned. "I didn't have chickens to feed and eggs to gather, but maybe my childhood was lacking not having a rural upbringing. I think giving my daughter this type of life will be wonderful. You can't change my mind, but I'm glad you are asking questions."

Beth sipped her meadow tea. *I wish Henry were here so he could see and hear how sincere Chloe seems about wanting us to be parents to her baby. I want to say yes, but I'm afraid Chloe will get married someday and then ask for her daughter. I can't raise her as mine for a few years only to lose her later.* "I have to be honest with you. Losing Nora Marie broke my heart. I'm afraid you might change your mind later. It can't be a temporary situation. I don't want to raise your daughter as my own and then you decide later that you made a mistake and take her away from me."

Chloe reached across the table and patted her arm. "I promise I won't do that. I've seen how hard losing Nora Marie has been on you. I never want you to lose another baby."

Beth twisted a lock of her long hair around her finger, embarrassed that she hadn't even brushed it yet. She wore her hair down instead of in a bun under her prayer covering. This had been the new norm for her with not going anywhere since Nora's death. She hadn't attended church with Henry because she felt too much pain. "I guess you've noticed how bad things have been here. I've had such a hard time dealing with people. You have definitely seen me at my worst. *Danki* for not giving up on me and for your kindness. Henry appreciated the food you brought."

"I'm sorry for your pain." Chloe ran her finger around the rim of her glass. "I have to tell you that I love how close your family is. Your mom and sisters have been here. When your dad was here, I noticed how he looked at you with so much love. My parents can't even come to visit me. That's when I realized how really close Amish families are and how much parents treasure their children."

"*Ya*, we are close. What did your parents say about you giving us your baby? Will they try to take her from us?"

Chloe laughed bitterly. "I'm sure they won't. I called today to tell my mom and dad my plans. My call went to Dad's voicemail and Mom couldn't talk long with me because she was busy. After I told Mom that I was giving her granddaughter to you and Henry, she said that was nice. Even if they try anything, it won't work. I'm eighteen. But honestly, I can't see them taking the baby from you."

When her cell phone rang, Chloe took it out of her bag. Glancing at the screen, she said, "It's Tony. He delivered a baby late last night."

Beth stood and walked to the refrigerator. Opening the refrigerator, she removed a pitcher of iced tea. She refilled her glass with the tea. *I'm surprised Chloe wants me to adopt her baby. Can I risk taking her child? I'm afraid to say yes.*

She couldn't help listening, and tensed when she heard Chloe's gasp, with words of sympathy following. What had happened that Chloe offered prayers for Tony's dad and family? She went to the sink to look out the window, hoping Henry was home. There was no sign of him, so she returned to the table, carrying her glass of iced tea. Chloe's phone wasn't in sight, so she asked, "Would you like more iced tea?"

Chloe rubbed her forehead. "No, *danki*, but it is delicious."

"*Ya*, we like it. I make it with our peppermint leaves."

"Tony called to tell me that his dad had a heart attack and is in the ICU unit. He's leaving now to drive to Cleveland. His parents live there."

Sitting again on the chair across from Chloe, Beth said, "I hope his dad will be okay."

"I offered to go with him and help drive, but he said I should stay here. Tony said that I might go into labor. He's probably afraid he'd have to stop too often at rest areas so I could go pee."

I wonder what Tony thinks about Chloe's new adoption plans, Beth thought. "You could start labor soon. I was surprised he bought a house in Fields Corner and decided to become a partner with Dr. Foster."

"Tony got the house for a good price. It was a hard decision for him. He's not enthusiastic about home births, but he's trying to keep an open mind about them. His dad is a family care physician. Fortunately, he shares his practice with a couple other doctors, so they can take care of Dr. Cunningham's patients until he can return to work."

"Did you mention to Tony about us raising your baby?" She might as well refer to Dr. Cunningham by his first name. *Chloe and the young doctor must be close,* Beth thought. *He called to let her know he was leaving town. It seems likely she might have talked to him about what she should do about her baby.*

"I started to last evening, but before I could finish telling him, he had to leave to deliver a baby. I didn't say anything now because he was in a hurry to leave to see his dad." Chloe leaned forward in her chair. "It doesn't matter what Tony thinks or what my family wants me to do. I have made my decision. I know my daughter will feel wanted from receiving a lot of support and love from you. The type of life you have in the Plain community is what I want for her." Chloe grinned. "Just think, we both have dark brown hair, and even Henry's lighter brown hair is the same color as Logan's. She'll even look like your daughter. And I'm sure you'll have more children, so she'll be a big sister to the children you will have someday."

Beth was so touched by Chloe's words that tears started spilling down her cheeks. It was a change to cry with happiness instead of with profound grief. Holding Chloe's newborn in her arms would be *wunderbaar,* and loving her would be easy.

What will Henry say? Will he think we should adopt Chloe's baby?

"I'll pray about it and I need to talk with Henry, but in my heart I already love her because she's part of you. I want to give your baby the life you want for her."

Chloe stood and walked around the table to Beth. Leaning down, she hugged her. "Thank you so much. It means the world to me that you want to do this. I hope you and Henry will be her parents."

Chapter Eighteen

Beth felt refreshed after taking a shower. Combing through her hair, she noticed how shiny it looked now. She wore a lavender dress with a matching apron. Rushing down to the kitchen, she hoped Henry would be home. Quickly, she glanced out the kitchen window and saw her husband walking away from the barn and toward their house. *Good, he's home now and I can tell him the big news.* She still couldn't believe that Chloe wanted them to be her baby's parents. *What if Henry doesn't agree to Chloe's plan? I'll have to convince him that it's the right thing to do.* More than anything, she wanted to be the mother to Chloe's daughter.

She couldn't wait another second, so hurried to open the screen door for Henry. She kissed his cheek and he pulled her into his arms. "I'm glad I left. You must've missed me." He fingered a lock of her hair. "You look pretty."

"*Danki.* After Chloe left, I took a shower."

Henry frowned slightly. "I thought she was coming this afternoon."

"*Nee*, it was this morning. I thought you realized it was in the morning."

"Maybe it's *gut* I wasn't here. You girls must have had a good chat. I like seeing you *froh.*"

"I have *wunderbaar* news." She thought about moving to the living room where they could get comfortable on the sofa, but decided to go ahead to share why Chloe had visited. "Chloe wants us to adopt her baby girl. I want this so much, Henry. Her baby will never take the place of our sweet Nora, but I think God brought Chloe into our lives for this purpose."

Henry raised his eyebrows. "Why would she want us to be parents to her child? Obviously we won't be giving her daughter the type of childhood she's had."

"That's why. She wants an Amish home for her baby because her parents have never put her first. A nanny raised her. She loves how close our families are. Chloe also wants a father and a mother for her child."

"There has to be an English couple able to give their love and attention to her daughter. I'm sure there are many fine couples who don't hire a nanny."

Beth saw worry clouding Henry's eyes. She rested her head against his chest, hearing his strong heartbeat. "Please pray about it. I want this baby so much."

"We plan on having many *kinner*. Will Chloe decide later that she doesn't like her daughter being part of our large family?"

"She mentioned her daughter being a big sister to our future children. Chloe promised she wouldn't change her mind. I believe her." Raising her head to look at Henry, she continued, "We have all the baby things we need, so we don't have to buy anything."

"We don't need to give Chloe an answer yet. She just mentioned it to you. We need to give this careful thought."

Seeing the indecision in her husband's eyes concerned Beth. *What will I do if Henry refuses to raise Chloe's baby as our own?*

* * *

Violet stood in the doorway of a room filled with paints, brushes, and canvases. She watched Luke's sister, Priscilla, paint her horse Murphy on a canvas resting on an easel. Although Violet wanted to talk to Priscilla, she hated to disturb her while she painted. Priscilla's lovely auburn hair was down her back, reaching her waist. Maybe it helped her creativity to have her hair loose instead of in a bun. Violet had noticed that Luke's sister never wore a prayer covering when she painted. Of course, there wasn't any reason to cover her hair inside the house with only two women around. Over her old dress, Priscilla wore a dark blue apron.

For the past several days, Luke's sister had stayed with her. When her mother was back in Kentucky and not staying with Violet at the farmhouse, Priscilla was happy to stay with her. No one seemed to want Violet to be alone. She wasn't sure if it was because her father was famous, and they worried that someone might break into the house while she was there alone. But really, if that was the reason, Violet doubted two women instead of one would stop someone from breaking into the house. Or it could be they were afraid Luke and she would be tempted to spend too much time together before their marriage.

When Priscilla was needed at home, Uncle David insisted that Matthew and Noah spent the nights with her. Violet thought they liked a break from the routine at home. Those twin brothers were always looking for new adventures, so it was fun to have them spend time with her. Their horse and pony races were especially exciting.

Priscilla turned her head to look at Violet. "What's up? Are you smiling because you like my picture?"

"I was thinking about Matthew and Noah and how I love beating them when we have our horse races. Murphy is such a fantastic horse." Violet stepped closer to the painting. "You have an amazing talent. I love that you are doing this painting for a wedding gift."

Violet knew some Old Order Amish districts frowned on art as being useless, but fortunately, Luke's father encouraged Priscilla to paint. Her paintings sold extremely well in some of the local stores and at school fundraisers.

Priscilla squinted her blue eyes. "I wanted to do something special for you. I'm excited you chose me to be one of your attendants. Do you want me to sew your wedding dress?"

"*Danki*, but my mom is going to. She could probably sew your dress if you want."

"I'll have time to do it. Your mother is so sweet. Are you disappointed that you can't wear a white gown like Eliza did for her wedding? I know you probably dreamed as a little girl to wear a white wedding dress."

Violet smiled. "I never thought that much about my wedding until I fell *in lieb* with Luke. I get to wear a white apron over my blue dress and white prayer *kapp*, so I'm excited about that. All the wedding details aren't as important to me as marrying Luke. I can't wait until we are husband and wife."

"That's *gut*. *Mamm's* definitely excited to sew Luke's wedding suit." Priscilla continued in a firm voice, "This is your chance to make demands of your attendants. Judith and I want to help you have the most beautiful and romantic wedding ever."

Violet grinned. "You might be sorry you offered after I give you a list of things I want done."

Priscilla waved her paintbrush. "I'm not worried. Hey, *Daed* is over the moon with you doing so well in the baptism classes."

Violet had been surprised at the peace and enjoyment she received from going to the instructional classes. "I'm glad he is."

"You know we all hope you and Luke will live with us after you're married."

"My parents said we could live here, and this does seem like home to me now . . . but we've also thought about living above the buggy shop. I'll be close to my work that way and won't have to drive a buggy to town." Violet still hadn't gotten used to driving places in a buggy instead of a car. Her grandparents, Esther and Jonas Troyer, had died in a buggy accident, and that had been a worry of hers when she sold her car and became committed to living as an Amish woman. However, she was getting better about it, and trusted the Lord to keep her safe in a buggy. It seemed being Amish definitely caused her to pray without ceasing. Living in the Plain community meant you couldn't drive a car or have electricity in your home. Because of these challenges, Violet thought her faith had been enriched. A simple life helped her to remain closer to God.

"If you and Luke change your minds, the invitation is always open. Just think, you would save time without having to cook daily for Luke. I think that's why *Mamm* enjoys teaching, because Anna and I take turns cooking during the school week."

Violet laughed. "I never thought of that. Of course, I have crazy hours with babies deciding to be born during the middle of the night, so I hate to disrupt the Kings' household with my midwife hours. It's another reason we might live in town at first."

Priscilla used a rag to wipe paint off the brush. "I'm going to take a break and get a glass of iced tea."

"Something cold sounds good. It's such a hot day." *It figures I have the day off on one of the hottest August days. Working in the air-conditioned hospital, office, and birthing center is a nice benefit.*

Violet walked ahead of Priscilla to the kitchen. Glancing out the window, she saw Beth tethering her horse to the post in the backyard. Opening the kitchen door, she yelled, "Hello, Beth. Come on in. We were just getting iced tea."

Beth gave a broad smile as she climbed the steps to the back porch. "*Mamm* told me you were home today. I have the most terrific news. Chloe came to see me this morning. She wants me to adopt her baby."

"What did you tell her?" Priscilla asked, standing in front of the sink. She stopped washing her hands for a moment to look over her shoulder at Beth.

"I told her I had to talk with Henry. He's not sure about it, but I am. I went to see *Mamm* before I came here. She said I need to realize that Chloe might change her mind someday, and knows it'll be hard for me not to get attached. *Mamm* told me I should pretend the baby is a foster child, so it won't be as painful if Chloe or her parents want the baby later."

Priscilla turned to face Beth, wiping her hands on a dishtowel. "It's interesting how you and Chloe both have dark brown hair and are about the same height. Chloe might be a bit taller. Her daughter might even resemble you."

Violet poured three glasses of iced tea and handed one to Beth. "Let's sit at the table. I'll get some cookies out for us."

"I decided to ask you what you think, Violet, about Chloe's offer." Beth sat on a chair and sipped her tea. "You've seen Chloe a lot for her prenatal visits. I believe she's serious about adoption."

Before sitting down, Violet put a plate of peanut butter cookies on the table. "Chloe has surprised me with her maturity. I think she had to grow up quickly with becoming pregnant."

"Logan hasn't been any support to her, and now he's broken up with her." Beth took a cookie. "I'm sure he won't care if we adopt the baby."

"She mentioned wanting to marry him so they could be a family," Violet said. "Chloe's probably sincere now about adoption, but when she holds her daughter in her arms she could change her mind."

I wonder what Tony thinks of Chloe's plan, but he might not be aware of it, Violet thought. *He's away in Cleveland with his family. Tony's face lights up whenever Chloe is near. I can see them becoming more serious after she gives birth. The age difference doesn't seem to matter to them. If they do continue seeing each other and Chloe remains in Fields Corner, will it be too hard on Chloe to see her baby in Beth's arms? Will she regret giving her baby away?*

"If Chloe decides to keep her baby, I'm sure you and Henry will have more *kinner.*" Priscilla gave Beth's shoulder a squeeze before she sat next to her.

"Maybe Henry and I will have more babies, but we can't be sure that will happen."

Violet raised her eyebrows at Beth. "There is no medical reason why you won't have future babies. And you don't have to worry about having another stillborn."

Beth nodded sadly. "I hope I'll never have another stillborn. I know it was hard on you, too, Violet."

Violet had never mentioned to Beth how seeing Nora had upset her so much that she had seriously considered not continuing as a nurse-midwife for future babies. She saw Beth more than the doctors did while she was pregnant. Had she missed something that might have saved Nora's life? After much thought and reading her notes, Violet realized that it wasn't her fault. She loved being a midwife and wouldn't quit now. "It was so unexpected and sad. Nora was such a beautiful baby."

"I look at the pictures each day that Chloe took of her." There was a faint tremor in Beth's voice as she became emotional.

Violet saw the pain flickering in Beth's eyes as she spoke. "I miss Nora all the time and no one will ever take her place. But I do believe with my whole heart that God wants me to adopt Chloe's daughter."

Chapter Nineteen

Although Chloe was exhausted on Tuesday evening after giving birth to her baby girl, she wanted to hold her as much as possible. Soon she'd be giving her to Beth, but for the next couple of days, she wanted to be alone with her daughter before she had to say goodbye. She hadn't called her friend about being in labor or that she'd given birth. *I'll call later tonight and leave a message on their phone.* Fortunately, Beth had stopped to see her on Monday morning to tell her that they'd be happy to raise her child as their own.

During the visit, Chloe mentioned loving the name Emma, and asked Beth what she thought of it. She'd told her, "I know I said I wasn't going to name the baby, but deep down I've always thought of her as Emma. If you have a name in mind, it's fine. It should be your choice and Henry's."

Beth smiled. "We'll call her Emma. It's a *wunderbaar* name."

Wearing a fresh hospital gown and sitting up in bed, she gazed with love at her little miracle. Many emotions raced through her mind, but she would not allow herself to cry. "I will concentrate on the little time we have to together, my baby girl," she whispered softly. "I wasn't going to give you a name myself, but I'm glad Beth agreed to the name that I love. You look like an Emma to me.

"Please, Father, give me the strength to give my daughter to Beth and Henry. It will be hard, but I love her too much to keep her," Chloe prayed. How could she ever give her infant the kind of life she deserved as a single mom without any home or income? *Look how alone I am now. Everyone's too busy to come see my baby. No one was with me during labor—well, Dr. Foster and Jennifer were, but no family.* It hurt deeply that her parents hadn't returned her phone calls. She knew they were busy with the TV people filming about the cancer center, but couldn't they spare a moment to call her back? She'd given birth to their first grandchild. Didn't that mean anything to them? Sure, she could tell herself that they didn't want to form any kind of a bond, since they believed strongly the best thing was for her not to raise their granddaughter.

She thought about calling Andrea or Carter, but realized they hadn't even bothered to visit her in Fields Corner. In fact, when she'd gone home, they hadn't made any attempt to see her. Aunt Angie drove her to the hospital, but she had to leave suddenly when there was a fire in the restaurant's kitchen. Fortunately, Tyler was with his dad, so her aunt didn't need to make arrangements for her son.

Chloe kissed Emma's forehead, wishing with her whole heart that things could be different, but she felt thankful to have a healthy daughter. "You are perfect. I hope someday you will know that my love for you is so powerful that I want you to have the best life ever. You will always be in my thoughts and prayers each day."

When she heard a slight knock on the door, Chloe thought of Tony, but it was silly to think it could be him. *He's still in Cleveland with his family.* With his dad still in ICU, Tony hadn't returned to Fields Corner. He'd texted and called her several times to give her updates about his father. *Funny, how I hear more from Tony than my own family. I'll text him a picture of the baby sometime soon. And Logan, too, even though he hasn't shown any interest in our daughter. He's the baby's daddy and should see a picture of his child.*

After a second knock sounded on the door, Chloe said, "Come in." When she saw her brother and dad enter the room, her jaw dropped. "I can't believe I'm actually seeing you two."

Carter moved quickly to the side of her bed. "We wanted to see you and your baby." Leaning closer to the baby, he stared at his niece. "She's beautiful."

Her head was spinning that some of her family had come to the hospital. Why had they ignored her texts about being in labor? She'd also left a couple phone messages. "Why didn't you answer my messages and tell me you planned on visiting? While I was in labor, I could've used some family support, or at least a mention that you were praying for me, or *some* kind of concern. But I didn't hear from my siblings or my parents. I know the TV crew was at the clinic today, but it wouldn't have killed you to make a quick call. At least Aunt Angie drove me here, so I didn't have to drive myself to the hospital. She only left because of a kitchen fire at the restaurant."

Her dad flinched. "I'm afraid something happened while the TV crew were taping at the cancer clinic. I didn't see your texts or calls until later today."

"What happened?" It was probably something that wasn't perfect enough for her mother, so she'd insisted everything had to be taped again.

Carter put his hand on their father's shoulder. "Dad, sit down."

It must be huge, because Dad looks haggard and stressed, she thought.

After her dad sat on a chair, he sucked in a deep breath. "Chloe, I had an affair. I broke it off months ago, but the woman showed up today at the clinic and made a scene. I'm not sure why Olivia decided to come to the clinic. She must've heard on the news about the cancer center being featured on a national network, and wanted to embarrass me and your mother."

Chloe had never in a million years expected to hear "affair" come out of her father's mouth. For a moment, she couldn't speak. "I can't believe you would cheat on Mom. I thought you two had a solid and happy marriage."

Her dad shook his head. "I have regretted each day what I did. Your mother and I went to counseling one evening a week during the last few months of your school year."

Suddenly, Chloe realized what she had thought was their date night was instead their therapy night with a marriage counselor. "I never suspected anything was wrong."

"With it being your senior year, we decided not to tell you about the problems we were having."

"Did you tell Carter and Andrea?"

He nodded. "We did, and we were going to tell you after graduation, but when we learned you were pregnant, your mom said we should wait. I agreed because I thought we could work things out."

"Who is this Olivia? How did you meet her?" Chloe couldn't remember anyone by the name of Olivia working at her father's law firm.

"She works as a paralegal at another firm. We met during a case. After the lawsuit was settled, we went to lunch. I wish I could do everything over," her father stammered.

Carter stopped gazing at the baby to stare at her. "Dad's been living with me in my condo."

"When you came home, I stayed at the house to keep the charade up. I slept in one of the other bedrooms. I'm sorry I haven't been a better father to you, Chloe." His voice quavered with sadness.

She remained quiet because what he'd said was true. He hadn't been a father to her for a long time. He'd been neglectful and distant, but he looked so broken to her now. A memory of him that was something she'd forgotten came to her. It was nice to remember now that when she was little and asleep, he used to carry her upstairs to her bedroom. She sometimes pretended to be asleep so he'd carry her in his arms. Even though her dad might have realized she wasn't asleep, he had held her tightly against him. Sometimes he murmured, "Chloe, you're my sweet little girl. I love you."

Chloe took his hand in hers and gave it a gentle squeeze.

"I've messed up big time. I love my wife and should never have been unfaithful to her. My law partners are angry at me because I've been having trouble focusing on my cases. Your mom is insisting on a divorce. I don't want one, but she wants to put the house on the market this month. She said it's time for us to go our separate ways, and selling the house is the first step."

"I'm sorry, Dad. I wish you and Mom had told me before, but I'm glad you did now. Everything makes a bit more sense to me. I kept wondering why you or Mom didn't offer to help me with the baby so I could keep her. I never realized you and Mom were having serious martial problems." Chloe wondered about the other woman, but decided not to ask her father anything about her. Although she was angry at her dad for cheating on her mom, she could see why it happened. Her mother was so absorbed in her clinic that he probably felt neglected. That was still no reason for him to be unfaithful, but she didn't need to tell him that. He'd already admitted he had been in the wrong and hadn't made any excuses for his adultery.

He frowned. "We argued about your baby a lot too. I thought we should tell you that we'd support you if you decided to keep the baby. But things have been so unsettled that I started thinking your mother's adoption suggestion was the best option."

"I was very disappointed that you and Mom didn't want me to keep the baby. I thought my bedroom at home was huge enough for me to put a baby bed in it, but after Logan broke up with me I knew adoption would be the best choice." Chloe stared at Emma, understanding now why she'd felt God wanted her to ask Beth and Henry to be the parents. He knew her parents' arguments and problems would not provide the best environment to raise her baby. "I want this precious baby to have a father and a mother." Raising her head to glance at her dad and Carter, she said, "I named her Emma. I talked to the adoptive mother and she agreed to call her Emma. She loves the name too."

Carter, leaning closer to the baby, asked, "Is it okay if I hold Emma?"

Chloe grinned. "I guess I'll let my big brother hold her." Pointing to a bottle on a tray pushed to the other side of her bed, she said, "You can use the sanitizer to rub into your hands. The nurse said anyone can hold her as long as they are healthy and use the sanitizer."

Carter immediately squirted the lotion onto a hand, then rubbed both hands together. As he put the sanitizer back on the tray, his eyes met hers. "I'm sorry I haven't offered to have you and the baby stay with me. Daphne said it wouldn't work with us getting married. She's afraid there wouldn't be enough room for you and the baby. If you change your mind about adoption, I know Aunt Angie would love to have you stay with her and Tyler."

"I loved her for making the offer, but it doesn't seem the right thing for me to do." Chloe wondered why now Carter and her father seemed to feel a sense of family when it came to her. She guessed actually seeing her precious daughter in person caused them to realize how she would never be a part of their family. "As hard as it is for me to give her up, I think it's the best decision."

He took the baby in his arms and asked, "How much does she weigh?"

"Eight pounds and three ounces. And she's twenty-two inches long, so she's a nice size," Chloe answered.

"Emma is adorable and looks like a little angel." Carter carefully sat on a chair by the window, and then kissed his niece's forehead.

Chloe's heart felt heavy seeing the tenderness in her brother's eyes. Each moment was filled with happiness that her brother had come to share this miracle of life with her, but it caused great pain at the same time. Her baby girl wouldn't grow up knowing her uncle, aunt, or grandparents. *If only everything could be different, and Logan hadn't stopped loving me.*

Chloe watched Carter with her daughter for a couple more minutes, then turned her head to look at her dad. "What do you think of your granddaughter?"

"She reminds me of you when you were born. Your mom and I thought you had the most exquisite and beautiful features." He ran his fingers through his gray hair. "I wish things were different. I'm not sure where I'm going to live. I can't continue staying at Carter's place. I don't want to live with the newlyweds. They need their own space."

Carter's eyebrows shot up. "Dad, there's no rush. We aren't getting married until January."

Chloe thought January didn't seem like a great month to get married, but Carter's fiancée, Daphne, wanted to save her parents money. The rates for her preferred reception place were considerably lower in January.

"We're going to stop and see Angie and Tyler before we go home." Her dad sighed. "I wish I could tell you when your mom is visiting, but as usual it's hard to pin down a time with her. She should be calling you sometime this evening."

"I want to spend another night here. I decided to hold my

daughter and spend another day with her before the adoptive parents arrive to take her. I hope Mom can come tomorrow and see Emma."

Chapter Twenty

"Emma's lucky to have you for a mother." Henry smiled as he brought his coffee cup to his mouth.

Enjoying a Saturday morning with Henry while feeding their baby brought Beth a great deal of happiness. Sure, she still had sad moments about losing Nora, but having Emma had given her life a new purpose. It'd been two months since Chloe had given Emma to her, and each day she gave thanks to God for Emma. It made no difference that she wasn't the birth mother. She couldn't love Emma any more than she already did.

"I love holding her. She's such a sweet baby." Beth placed the empty baby bottle on the kitchen table, and then lifted Emma to her shoulder to burp her. After she patted the baby's back for a few moments, Emma burped. "Even hearing her cute burp gives me pleasure. I'm blessed to be Emma's mother."

Henry gave her a broad grin. "Do you feel blessed during the night feedings? I heard you at one o'clock mumbling you couldn't wait until she sleeps through the night."

"*Ach*, I'm sorry. I didn't mean to wake you up."

"It's fine. I went back to sleep quickly, but I should've gotten up with Emma. You need your sleep."

"You got up with her the last several nights while working hard each day."

"But you're pregnant. I don't mind getting up with Emma," Henry insisted.

She shrugged. "I don't remember feeling this tired when I was carrying Nora. And my morning sickness is worse this time. I'll be glad when the first trimester is over." Maybe she was carrying a boy this time, and that was the reason for severe morning sickness.

Henry leaned down and took Emma in his arms. He kissed the baby's forehead. "You're taking care of a newborn now, so that's probably why you're more exhausted this time. You should take a nap this morning, and another one this afternoon when Emma is sleeping. You look tired."

Seeing her husband with his huge hands holding tiny Emma against his chest made her realize what a precious picture it would make. Sometimes she wished her faith allowed photos.

She shook her head. "Emma and I are going to the school fundraiser today. They didn't make as much at the August one because of the stormy weather. I'll be there all day." Seeing Henry's look of concern, she wanted to convince him not to worry. "I promise I won't overdo it. I'll buy sandwiches there to bring home for supper. We have potato salad left over from yesterday. And I'll fix corn on the cob, so that's easy too."

"I'll agree for my two favorite girls to leave me if you will bring home one of Rachel Weaver's butterscotch pies."

She rolled her eyes at him. Henry loved to kid her about never making him a butterscotch pie. She personally didn't make that kind because she feared hers wouldn't be as good as Rachel's. "If she doesn't have butterscotch, what's your second choice?"

He grinned. "Surprise me. I'll hitch the buggy for you when you're ready to go."

"Violet's picking me up, so you don't need to do that."

"I wonder if *Mamm's* helping with the fundraiser too. She might be there to help with Emma. She certainly loves her a lot too. I wonder how many more clothes she's going to make for our baby."

Beth laughed. "I think you'll have to make another chest of drawers to hold everything. Your mother loves her granddaughter a lot, that's for sure."

He walked to the sink and rinsed his cup before placing it down on the counter. It was interesting how her husband had adapted to feeling secure enough to hold their baby in one arm while he used his other one to multitask. *He's such a wonderful father,* she thought.

He smoothed Emma's hair where it stuck up a little. "I love her dark hair. It looks just like yours."

"Everyone's amazed how much hair she has already."

Although it was true Emma had dark brown hair like hers, Chloe also had the same hair. At the hospital, Dr. Parrish had mentioned how Chloe and her sister both were born with lots of dark hair. Then Andrea lost her baby hair, and when it grew back in, it was blonde. Would Emma's hair be blonde someday like her aunt's and grandma's? And how long would it take her to stop thinking about Emma's birth family?

"Emma's sleeping. Should I put her in the crib upstairs?"

Beth shook her head. "You can put her in the Rock 'n Play Sleeper. I'm glad you brought it down this morning for me." She loved the Rock 'n Play Sleeper because it was just the right size to keep Emma conveniently by her side and was a great baby item to have. She liked how the sleeper had a headrest and newborn insert to help Emma to feel secure. *Or rather make me feel safe putting her in it*, she thought.

After he put their baby down, Henry said, "I better get to work. *Danki* for breakfast. It was *appeditlich*."

"If you really want to thank me, give me a kiss before you go outside," she teased. Henry always gave her a kiss before he went outside to work, but she felt flirty and carefree this morning. It was going to be a great day with taking Emma to the fundraiser and being with friends and family. But Henry, the love of her life, was the main reason for her joyfulness.

Remembering their earlier cuddling and loving each other in their cozy bed had been *wunderbaar*. There had been no morning sickness for a change, so she hadn't hesitated in giving herself freely to her husband.

Henry gently touched her cheek. The warmth of his hand gave her a pleasant rush. Seeing the love in his eyes made her even happier. He bent down, his lips found hers, and he deepened his kiss for several moments. She kissed him back with the same fervor.

Once he broke their kiss and grabbed his straw hat off the peg, Beth stood and said, "I'll see you later."

Henry plopped his hat on his head. "I hope my girls have a good day."

"We will." After the screen door slammed shut behind him,

she whispered to Emma, "I'm glad Daddy didn't wake you with his noisy exit."

While her baby slept, she washed the few breakfast dishes. She wanted to get the diaper bag ready before Violet came. She needed to get several bottles filled with formula, since Emma liked to be fed every three hours. What a shame she couldn't have had Emma earlier, so she could've attempted breastfeeding her adopted child. She decided to use the disposable diapers instead of the cloth ones. Emma wouldn't need to be changed as often at the fundraiser that way. *I might as well use the Pampers Chloe bought before Emma gets too big for the small size. Chloe gave them the diapers when they went to the hospital to get the baby.*

She sighed, thinking about her English friend. *Only Chloe seemed to understand my depression. Molly and* Mamm *were sympathetic, but never could grasp why weeks after Nora's death, my grief kept me in a darkness that I couldn't climb out of. But Chloe knew what would jolt me back to the living. With her big heart, she realized having Emma would help me to be part of life again. Of course, Molly and her mother couldn't give her a baby to raise, but they had been uncomfortable around her. Amish women are supposed to be strong and to accept whatever God gave them.*

When Chloe gave me Emma, my life turned around. I couldn't seem to let go of my sadness until I became a mother to this sweet baby.

Beth felt certain that the present pregnancy was a result of her optimistic change in attitude. Raising *kinner* was such an important part of Amish life, so when she lost Nora she didn't care about anything. Her depression over Nora's death took so much out of her. She couldn't imagine going through another pregnancy, because it would be too hard to hope the next baby would not be stillborn. Why should the next baby be healthful? She thought before Chloe gave birth to Emma.

Once she had Emma in her arms, she regained her zest for everything. She could be a wife to Henry again, and their lovemaking took on a new closeness and urgency. When she first suspected a baby had been implanted in her womb, she'd bought a pregnancy test. Why bother Violet when she could see firsthand if she was pregnant or not?

Even though Chloe mentioned that it would be nice for her daughter to have younger siblings someday, I doubt she wanted it to happen this soon. I want to keep my pregnancy a secret from Chloe for as long as possible. Outside of Henry, only Violet knows I'm pregnant, but soon I'll have to go in for prenatal visits. I don't want Tony to learn about us expecting a baby yet. I know he's been driving to Cincinnati to see Chloe. I'm sure he'd tell her if he knew. If he hadn't been away when Chloe went into labor, would he have tried to talk her out of giving Emma to us?

During the first few weeks with her baby, she worried Chloe's mother would come and take her granddaughter away from them. When they met her at the hospital, Dr. Parrish looked disappointed at Chloe's choice. It must have seemed strange to the famous doctor that her daughter chose Amish parents instead of English ones.

What if Chloe decides to take Emma away from us because I'm already pregnant? I can't lose Emma. After she finished wiping off the countertop, Beth glanced at her sleeping baby. *I'm being too paranoid. Chloe would never do this to us. It seems she's moved on with her life anyhow. I'm relieved she never calls or writes to check on Emma. Well, she did check once to ask about Emma, but that was weeks ago. Nothing since.*

* * *

After the two women took a Saturday morning run together, Chloe made Belgian waffles while her mom fixed the coffee and bacon. They decided to take their plates of food outside to the deck. The October weather was lovely, with the temperatures being in the sixties.

"Thanks for taking it easy on me this morning and slowing your running pace." Her mom grinned at her.

"Hey, I'm impressed with your running." Her mother was sixty-two years old but never seemed that age to Chloe. She'd always had a youthful air to her, and wore her dyed blonde hair in a chin-length style. Chloe remembered her mom saying once how having her at age forty-four had kept her young. She guessed it must have been a big deal to have a baby at an older age when her mother thought her childbearing years were over.

Her mom swallowed a mouthful of waffle. "This is delicious.

Best waffle I've ever tasted."

Chloe smiled at her mom. "I got the recipe from Jeremy. He's the cook at Aunt Angie's restaurant. He enjoyed teasing me and giving me a hard time when I asked him for it. He said it was a family recipe, and he'd have to get permission first to give it to a Cincinnati girl."

"I'm glad you got the recipe." Her mom sipped her coffee and gave her a thoughtful look. "Angie bragged on you a lot and how great you did at the restaurant. She also said how much you helped her with taking care of Tyler. But sometimes I think that your dad and I made a mistake making you leave home for the summer."

"At first I thought you and Dad made a mistake too, but I'm glad now you did."

"I never thought of you meeting and dating someone like Tony because of the age difference. I have to admit, you two seem to belong together."

Chloe gave a small laugh. "In the beginning, I thought you asked Dr. Foster to hire Tony so he could keep tabs on me."

Her mom frowned. "I never would do something like that. I didn't know Tony until you introduced us."

Chloe broke off a piece of bacon. "I'll blame my pregnant brain for thinking something so ridiculous."

"Why don't you visit Beth today so you can see Emma? I know you want to see her." Her mom reached across the patio table and patted her arm. "I'm sorry I encouraged you to give her away. It's hard seeing you still sad, and I heard you crying again last night. I believed it was for the best for you not to keep Emma, but when I hear you sobbing for her, it breaks my heart."

Chloe didn't reply for a moment, wishing she could have kept Emma. Giving her away was the hardest thing she had ever done, and living each day without her baby broke her spirit and heart. A lump began to swell in her throat, and her appetite completely left her. "Mom, I can't visit them. I do want to see her, but I'm afraid what I'll do if I see Emma. I'm not strong enough to leave without her again. I constantly want to hold her and have her in my life. Even though it's been a couple of months, I still want her so much."

"I hate to bring this up again, but I still don't understand why you chose Beth to be Emma's adopted mother. I thought you were going to have Karen and Jeff adopt her. They can't have children. I know you said it seemed she'd have a better home life with Beth and Henry, but why choose an Amish family when you had other choices?"

Chloe remembered the day her mother came to the hospital to see Emma. She'd been surprised when Chloe told her that Amish parents were her choice. *Mom hadn't been paying attention the day I told her my decision.* It'd hurt her that once again the clinic had been more important to her mother than anything else. She hated that her dad had had an affair, but it seemed Mom had to take some responsibility for their marriage falling apart.

Chloe stiffened, recalling how disappointing it'd been to hear Karen, the mother she wanted for Emma, complain about the Amish. "Karen made negative comments about Amish people. It bothered me to hear her prejudice while I lived in the Plain community. I respect their way of life. When I realized Logan was definitely not going to be a father to Emma, I had to give her to a stable couple. Henry and Beth will raise her in a Christian home. And it's also like I said before, that Beth lost her baby. I felt God wanted me to give Emma to Beth and Henry. End of story." To her own ears, she sounded irritated, but it was too hard to talk about her decision. *I haven't been able to call Beth again to ask about Emma. Calling during my first week home was painful. Well, it's hard to connect with Beth without her having a cell or landline phone in their house.* The one time she'd called was when the time was arranged through Violet.

Her mom's brow wrinkled. "I'm sorry for everything, Chloe."

"I know you are, Mom." Chloe knew what her mother meant—she was apologizing for not being supportive about her keeping Emma.

"It seemed so many things happened when you told us you were pregnant. Your dad and I had just started going to marriage counseling because I was in a bad way due to his affair. I never thought he would cheat on me. I always thought we had a good marriage. It hurt me so much, but I realize now it was my fault too. I didn't give enough attention to our marriage. During the same time, my close friend, Jean, died when her cancer came back. Then you shocked us with being pregnant."

Looking closely at her mother's face, Chloe noticed the compassion in her gaze. Then she saw the dark circles under her eyes. *I'm not the only one not sleeping well. Apparently Mom is having trouble too.* For her parent to apologize about Emma and then to confess that some of the responsibility was hers for a failed marriage was huge. In the past, her mother was confident and seldom apologized for any of her decisions.

Although Chloe could've started college in August, as she physically felt fine, she wasn't emotionally ready. Since she hadn't felt like taking any college courses, Chloe had gone to work at the cancer clinic. Seeing her mother in action was amazing. When many of the patients talked of beating cancer because of Dr. Parrish's skill, Chloe understood why it was important to her mother to devote her time to sick patients.

Maybe it's time to forgive my mom, Chloe thought as she sipped her coffee. *I have her to thank for meeting Tony. If I hadn't gone to Dr. Foster for my prenatal care, I never would have met my boyfriend. Unlike Logan, he's a wonderful and mature guy. I can't imagine life without Tony.*

"Mom, I forgive you, and know you were acting in my best interests. Because of your decision, I met Tony. And I'm glad I'm not away at college with Logan. I've enjoyed working at your clinic and seeing how you make a positive difference in people's lives. And Andrea has impressed me too."

Tears glistened in her mother's eyes. "I've loved having you at the clinic. Andrea has commented on how grown-up you are. She's also enjoyed working with you."

Chloe smiled. "You two have been ingenious in finding various jobs for me to do."

"Hey, our receptionist did go on vacation and we didn't have to hire a temp. And you assisting in varied capacities has helped a lot."

"What about the coffee? Do I really make the best java?" Andrea praised her coffee, so she made it daily. What Chloe didn't say was that keeping busy at the clinic had kept her sane. Working long hours with her mother helped her to get through each day without Emma.

But the nights were terrible, and many times she was tempted to drive to Fields Corner to spend time with her baby. *Maybe I'll go sometime this month, but I don't think I can risk it yet. Even though I feel God wanted me to give Emma to Beth, I still have this strong maternal yearning to take her back. And that terrifies me. What if I can't stop missing my little girl?*

Chapter Twenty-One

"*Danki* for picking me up." Beth said, as she climbed into the buggy.

"I'm happy to have the company." After Violet stowed the stroller and diaper bag in the back of the seat, she joined Beth and Emma in the front seat. Violet picked up the reins and set the buggy into easy motion. Soon they left the driveway, and she steered the horse onto a rural road.

"It's such a beautiful fall day. I hope a lot of people come to this fundraiser."

Violet grinned. "My mom and several of her friends from their prayer group are coming, so that's already some guaranteed big sales."

"That's wonderful." Beth smiled at Violet, noticing strands of her dark brown hair peeking out from beneath her white prayer *kapp*. She wondered if Violet had quickly done her hair before going to work. She knew Violet sometimes went to the office on Saturday morning to meet Ada, the other midwife in their district. They liked to have the quieter Saturday mornings to review all their patient files and talk about any future pregnancy problems.

Of course, sometimes that didn't make a difference. The midwives and doctors had never seen anything to worry about during her first pregnancy with Nora. Something must've occurred late to cause her baby to die. *Maybe we should have had an autopsy to determine the cause.* Immediately, she decided it was *gut* they hadn't done it. It wouldn't have brought Nora back, and maybe they wouldn't have learned anything.

Violet turned her head to glance at Emma. "She looks so cute in her pink dress."

"Henry's mother made the dress and matching bonnet. She loves having a granddaughter."

"There's nothing like a grandmother's love." Violet grinned at her. "I think it's because they realize how pleasant it is to just enjoy grandchildren and not have to worry about having them full-time . . . like when they had their own children."

"I'm glad they love Emma. Even *Daed* loves holding her. After all his opposition to us mingling too much with the English, he doesn't seem to care now that he has a granddaughter whose birth parents were English."

"*Were* is the difference. You and Henry are now Emma's parents."

"I hope Chloe won't be upset that I'm pregnant already."

"She had to know you would want more children." Violet's eyes filled with concern. You seem like you're feeling better today. Are you?"

"It's been a better morning. I think your suggestion to eat ginger snaps or drink ginger tea has helped some. And I'm eating several light meals. I'm relieved I'm not feeling nauseous, because I didn't want to miss the fundraiser. I've had severe morning sickness most days, though. It's been a surprise to feel nauseous, because I seldom felt sick with Nora."

"When my Aunt Irene was pregnant with Matthew and Noah, she had severe morning sickness during the first three months. From my classes, I've learned this sometimes happens when there are twins. Also you mentioned being exhausted all the time and having to take naps whenever Emma does. You're six weeks pregnant, so I think you should have an ultrasound next week. Let's see if you might be carrying twins. I'll schedule it for next week."

"*Ach,* I can't imagine having twins so soon with already having one baby." Beth looked at Emma in her arms, wondering if it could be possible that she was carrying twins. How would she manage with three babies?

Violet gave her an apologetic look. "I didn't mean to worry you. You might not be carrying twins. Some women have severe morning sickness when carrying one baby."

Remembering the hospital expense from delivering Nora, she knew it would be hard to pay a second high bill. "If I am in the family way with twins, will I have to go to the hospital? I want to do what's best for the babies, but going to the hospital again will be expensive for us."

"It's possible to have a home birth with twins. Ada has delivered twins at home, and I remember Aunt Irene had Matthew and Noah at home. I'll schedule an appointment for you to see Dr. Foster soon."

"But remember I don't want Chloe to know I'm pregnant yet."

Violet arched her eyebrows. "Seeing the doctor won't cause Chloe to learn you're expecting."

"I'm afraid Tony will tell her. I want to keep it a secret as long as I can. I'm sure the longer I have Emma, the less chance I have of Chloe wanting to take her back."

"It'll be fine. Chloe isn't going to take Emma from you when she learns you're pregnant."

"I hope you're right. I don't want to lose her." Beth kissed Emma's forehead, taking a sniff of her sweet baby smell. "I did feel bad at the last fundraiser when Karen Gibson held Emma. She told me that she was supposed to be the adopted mother, but Chloe had changed her mind at the last minute. Karen had tears in her eyes and said how she and her husband had looked forward to being Emma's parents."

Violet's brown eyes widened. "I didn't know that. I'm sorry about Karen, but Chloe chose you and Henry. I'm sure she gave it a lot of thought and realized you should be Emma's mom."

Although she hoped Violet was correct, Beth knew deep down Nora's death and her depression had made Chloe change her mind. "I hope Karen gets a chance to be a mother. She seemed like a very nice woman. She must think another pregnant woman might choose her someday, because she bought a baby quilt at the last fundraiser."

* * *

Beth glanced at Emma in the stroller, and knew she'd fall asleep soon after a full belly of milk. She wondered if it would be a good time to use the restroom inside the school building. For the past three hours, she had been under a white canvas tent selling Priscilla's paintings and quilts made by several different Amish women. From the first moment she and Violet had arrived at the school, crowds of people had swarmed the whole area. Not only were the English customers buying the quilts and paintings, but they were also purchasing jams, bread, pies, cookies, noodles, cheese, and lunch meat. *It looks like many English families will be enjoying Amish food for their evening meals,* Beth thought.

Looking to see where Priscilla was, she noticed the *sold* signs on Samuel Weaver's pieces of furniture that were located outside the tent. Next to his spot were scattered picnic tables filled with customers enjoying hot sandwiches and side dishes. *All of us are benefitting from this huge turnout for our fundraiser.*

Although she didn't see Priscilla, Beth noticed Violet chatting with Carrie by a picnic table. *If I don't find Priscilla, maybe Violet can watch Emma and handle the sales.*

"How's my favorite niece?" Sadie asked as she peeked at Emma.

Beth chuckled. "She's your only niece."

"She's the cutest baby, but don't tell Molly I said that. She won't like that I said Emma is cuter than Isaac. I think girls are cuter than boy babies anyhow. I hope I have a baby just like Emma someday."

"I won't tell Molly your opinion. Come closer. Your hair is coming out of your *kapp,* which, by the way, is crooked. What have you been doing?"

Sadie rolled her eyes. "I played hide and seek with my friends."

Beth tucked her sister's auburn hair back underneath her prayer covering before straightening it. "There, now you look more presentable for a bishop's daughter."

"That's *gut.* I wouldn't want to disappoint *Daed.*"

Beth grinned at Sadie. "We both know that you're his favorite daughter, so I doubt you'd be in too much trouble. Could you watch Emma while I go to the restroom? She's going to fall asleep soon. I just fed her. I'll go first to find Priscilla to take care of the customers."

Sadie shook her head. "You don't need to get someone to

help. I can watch Emma and do the store part."

"I'm sure you can, but I'll still tell Priscilla I'll be gone for a few minutes." Beth leaned down and gave Emma a kiss on her cheek. "Be a good baby for your *Aenti* Sadie."

After she stood quickly, a wave of dizziness hit her and she grabbed the corner of the table. *Maybe it's because I was sitting too long.* As she slowly walked to locate Priscilla, an attractive woman with blonde hair approached her. "Did you make any of these quilts?"

"*Ya,* I made two of them."

The woman edged closer to the quilts "I'll show you the one I love, but I need it done in different colors."

"Which one do you love?" *Please don't be one of my quilts. I feel too lightheaded to concentrate, but I don't want to lose a sale. The school needs the money.*

The woman gestured toward a quilt on the end of a table. "It's the one with the navy-blue stars."

Beth blinked her eyes, realizing something was not right. With her head spinning, she said, "I'm sorry, but I'm not feeling well."

She sank to the floor and everything went black.

Chapter Twenty-Two

Before she opened her eyes, Beth heard several worried voices. Feeling dazed, she realized they were talking about her. Blinking, she saw the ground before strong arms turned her to her back. Gazing up at Violet, Beth asked, "What happened?"

"Beth, you fainted. Don't try to get up yet," Violet said. "Sadie, raise Beth's legs about a foot. When you fainted, your forehead must have hit the table or something. It looks like you have a small cut."

As Violet hovered over her, Carrie Robinson unscrewed a bottle of water and poured some of it on a cloth. "Here, use this to clean the cut. I have your bag here. Do you want me to get a bandage out for her wound?"

"Yes, and I have a tube of medicated ointment in there. Squirt some of it on a bandage."

"I thought you said it's a small cut," Beth murmured.

Violet nodded. "It is, but it's still bleeding a little."

"Sadie, is Emma okay?" Beth asked, while Violet applied the bandage to her forehead.

In a startled voice, Sadie said, "I ran here to see if you were okay. I'll go get her. I left Emma in the stroller."

Carrie held a bottle of water. "Beth, take a few sips of water. When was the last time you ate?"

"I ate a banana about an hour ago." Beth struggled to sit up because she wanted to see Emma. "How long was I out?"

"Less than a minute," Violet said. "Sit up slowly."

"You gave us a scare. Have you been feeling ill?" Priscilla squatted beside her, and her eyes were filled with concern.

"I feel fine now. I need to get up and take care of my baby," Beth said, after sitting still for a few seconds.

Sadie ran to her side and cried, "Emma's not in the stroller."

"She has to be, Sadie. I left her in the stroller with you," Beth said sharply. She stood up and ran to the baby carriage.

When she reached the empty stroller, her fingers touched the padded seat. Beth's stomach clenched as fear surrounded her heart. *Where could Emma be? She can't be missing.* She screamed, "Has anyone seen my baby girl? Please help me look for her."

Instantly, Priscilla joined her and asked Sadie, "Was there anyone near the stroller when you left Emma?"

Sadie shook her head. "I don't think so. I heard the commotion when Beth fainted and ran to see what happened."

"Why didn't you grab Emma when you checked on me?" Beth asked.

Sadie's voice broke and tears ran down her face. "I'm sorry. I wasn't thinking and was worried about you."

"We need to quickly look for Emma." Carrie touched Priscilla's shoulder. "You go into the school building and see if someone took her there to your mother. Someone might have gone to tell Lillian that Beth was ill and tried to be helpful by taking Emma."

After Priscilla left, Violet asked Beth, "Do you think Beverly could have picked Emma up?"

"She ended up staying home to watch my sister-in-law's sick sons. They have chicken pox. I guess that's why Beverly didn't offer to keep Emma with her. I should've stayed home with Emma. We have to find her." Panic seared along Beth's nerves, and she fought to contain it.

Violet touched Sadie's shoulder. "You go to the playground and see if any of the children saw anyone with Emma."

"Okay, Violet." Sadie gave Beth a sad glance before she rushed away.

"I see my nephews. Maybe they saw someone with Emma. They've been helping Samuel with his customers." Carrie gestured to Matthew and Noah and yelled, "Come here."

As Beth watched the twins run to their aunt, she hoped and prayed that Matthew or Noah had seen her baby.

Carrie looked serious as she stared at both boys. "Beth's baby is missing. Have you seen Emma?"

"We didn't see Emma," Matthew said, "but we heard a baby cry when we helped Samuel carry a table to a van."

Noah frowned. "I didn't see much of the baby. But it looked like the mother put the baby in a car seat. The woman shut the car door quickly and clutched a pink blanket with one hand. When she saw me looking at her car, she glared at me and said, 'My baby's fine. I'm a good mother.'"

"Did you recognize the woman?" Carrie asked.

"*Nee.*" Noah nervously ran his fingers through his hair. "It was weird, because she wore a *kapp* and Amish clothing, but she quickly drove the car away."

Matthew nodded. "She hit the accelerator so hard that some gravel flew up in the air."

When Beth saw her mother approaching her with empty hands, her shoulders tensed and tears rimmed her eyes. "I was hoping Emma was with you. *Mamm*, who would take a tiny baby out of a stroller?"

"I don't see how this happened," her mother said. "Priscilla said you fainted, so was the kidnapper watching for a perfect moment to take Emma? And why take her?"

Violet lifted her phone out of her bag. "I'm going to call the police."

"*Ach*, you think that woman the boys saw must have kidnapped my baby, don't you? And the pink blanket Beverly made for Emma is gone. She must've picked up the blanket to keep her covered." Beth felt a twisting sensation in her gut. What kind of a sick person would kidnap her baby? She clutched Noah's hand. "Did you notice anything about her? What did she look like?"

"She had brown hair and wore a purple dress and apron," Noah said.

"She looked too old to be in her *rumspringa*." Matthew squinted his blue eyes. "I told Noah that she shouldn't be driving a car at her age when she was Amish."

Carrie glanced at Violet. "We need to get this information to the police. She obviously just left a few minutes ago. What did her car look like? Did you notice her license plate?"

"It was a white car." Matthew rubbed his forehead. "I can't remember any numbers, but noticed an E and N before the stones flew in the air."

Beth started to sob, and her knees buckled. Lillian grabbed her daughter before she fell to the ground.

Carrie said, "We'll get an AMBER Alert out right away. Beth, we'll find Emma."

* * *

Later in the afternoon, Tony called Chloe because he hadn't wanted her to hear it first on the news. He explained to her how Emma was snatched during the school fundraiser, and how the local police had searched the schoolyard and the road. Next, they planned to combine forces with the federal and state authorities to launch a massive search for Emma. When he said an AMBER Alert had been issued, Chloe cried, imagining how some evil person had taken her baby.

While she was still on the phone with Tony, her mother asked what was going on. After Chloe gave her mother the sad news, she immediately called Ted Malone, an FBI agent. She had treated his wife successfully at the cancer clinic and wanted his expert help in finding her granddaughter. While Chloe cried, her mom quickly called Angie to see if she knew more about the kidnapping.

After making arrangements with Andrea about the clinic, Carter and her dad came to the house to drive them all to Fields Corner. While on the highway, Chloe texted the woman in charge of their church prayer chain. She wanted prayers said that Emma would not be harmed and would be found soon.

By early evening, Beth and Henry Byler's house was filled with the police, FBI, and a detective. Also present were Amos, Lillian, Chloe, and her parents.

Chloe followed Beth upstairs to see where Emma had lived for the last two months. When Chloe asked if she could go upstairs to see Emma's things, Beth gave her a surprised expression. Then agreed to show her.

Once inside the master bedroom, Chloe touched the cradle

and said, "I take it that Emma still slept in your room." At Beth's nod, she asked, "Did Emma wake up a lot during the night?"

"Usually around one o'clock."

Beth's answer startled her. "That's so strange, because I've been waking up at that time. I guess a mother's bond with her baby exists even when separated by miles." Chloe swallowed hard and stared at Beth. "You seemed shocked that I would come here. I've missed Emma each day. I've kept it together by working long hours at my mother's clinic."

Beth crossed her arms roughly over her chest. "If you missed her so much, why didn't you call to ask about her? You only called once, and that was the first week after you left the hospital."

"It's a little difficult to call someone when they don't have a phone in the house."

"You managed to call me when we were both pregnant."

"We had scheduled times so you would be at your phone shanty. I wouldn't be that inconsiderate to make you go to the shanty when you had a baby to take care of." Chloe exhaled a deep breath. "Besides, I couldn't call or come see Emma because I knew I couldn't leave without her again. Ever since I've left Fields Corner, each day has been a struggle. I've yearned to hold Emma in my arms. Tony has been visiting me in Cincinnati because I knew I could never return here yet." Chloe gripped the cradle hard. "My mom suggested I visit this weekend and go to the fundraiser. I wish now I had and—"

Beth interrupted her, "Stop right there. I suppose if you had been at the fundraiser, you think Emma would never have been kidnapped. I can't help it that I fainted."

"I'm sorry, I didn't mean to upset you. I don't know if my being here would have helped, but it might have made a difference. Maybe I would've been holding Emma when you fainted." Chloe cleared her throat. "Tell me the truth, Beth— haven't you been glad I've given you the space to be Emma's mother without my interference?"

Leaning against her dresser, Beth nodded. "I have been glad. But I also thought maybe you had moved on with your life, since I hadn't heard from you. I love Emma so much."

Chloe wanted to ask her, *If you love my baby so much, why did you leave her with a little girl when many strangers were at the fundraiser?* Instead she said, "I was surprised to hear you're pregnant."

"I guess you overheard my *mamm* ask me if I could be pregnant." Beth fingered her white *kapp's* ties. "*Ya.* I'm pregnant. Emma will have a brother or sister."

Chloe had heard the two women talk in the kitchen about Beth's pregnancy, and that this time, she had severe morning sickness. She moistened her lips with the tip of her tongue, noting that Beth was clearly reminding her that Emma would continue to be part of their Amish family. "I knew you'd someday have more children, but I wasn't expecting it to happen so soon."

Beth shrugged. "I wasn't either, but I'm happy about this pregnancy. Henry and I want to have a large family. Remember, you told me that it'd be nice for Emma to be a big sister to our other children."

Chloe wasn't surprised that Beth brought up what she'd said earlier. "Congratulations on your pregnancy. I guess it's been hard on you taking care of a newborn while being pregnant and getting up for night feedings. Did Violet think that was why you fainted?"

"Many pregnant women faint," Beth said in a defensive tone of voice. "I'm sure getting up sometimes during the night didn't cause me to faint. Some nights Henry gets up with Emma. He loves our daughter a lot."

Beth senses I want Emma back. How could she not realize I feel I made a huge mistake? She wanted more than anything to tell Beth that when Emma was found—and she had to be found—that she wanted her baby back. She'd entrusted her child with Beth, and now some crazy woman had stolen Emma. But it wasn't the time to attack each other—what both of them needed was to pray together. She thought of the passage Matthew 18:20: "Where two or three are gathered in my name, there am I in the midst of them."

"I'm hoping Emma will be found soon, but the longer she's missing, the harder it will become. I think we should say a prayer together." Chloe moved away from the cradle to stand beside Beth.

"*Ya*, you're right. We need to pray."

Once they joined their right hands, Chloe said, "Our heavenly Father, please help that someone will recognize Emma and realize she's the baby who has been kidnapped today. And immediately the person will call the police, so that the kidnapper and Emma can be located. Keep Emma safe until she's found." Chloe paused to give Beth a chance to add to the prayer.

Beth continued, "We give thanks for the many people who are trying to find Emma and give them the guidance they need to locate her. We pray in Jesus' name, amen."

Chapter Twenty-Three

As Chloe entered the living room, she noticed a man who appeared to be in his fifties and had gray hair. Her mother introduced him as Agent Malone. He'd arrived while she and Beth were in the upstairs bedroom. He sat on the couch beside her parents while others were scattered throughout the big room. As more people had come to the Bylers' residence, Henry brought in chairs from the kitchen.

Agent Malone looked up from his notepad. "Mrs. Byler, your mother mentioned a Karen Gibson talked to you at a previous school fundraiser. Did you see this woman at today's fundraiser?"

Beth shook her head. "I never saw her today."

"You don't think she could've kidnapped Emma, do you?" Chloe asked Agent Malone. She couldn't imagine Karen resorting to stealing her baby. "She couldn't possibly think she'd get away with it."

"Karen Gibson could have hired a woman to do it and planned to get Emma later." Agent Malone tapped his pen against his pad. "She and her husband are wealthy and would have the resources to relocate later with your baby."

Chloe asked Beth, "What did Karen say to you?"

"I felt sympathy for her because she mentioned how you had chosen her to be Emma's mother, and then you changed your mind. I'm sure she came to see Emma." Beth had a thoughtful expression. "Why did you change your mind?"

"She made negative remarks about the Amish," Chloe said. "It bothered me that she would be judgmental. I decided then I didn't want someone like her to adopt Emma."

Beth smoothed her apron over her dress. "I did notice she bought a baby quilt, so I thought at the time maybe she was expecting to adopt another baby. Her sister was with her and she bought several things. Both women seemed nice."

"I think we can rule out ransom." Agent Malone glanced at Chloe's mother and said, "When you called me to help with this investigation, my first thought was that there would be a ransom call."

"I thought of that briefly too." Her mother gave a sad smile to Lillian and Amos. "I wish we could have met under different circumstances."

"I do too." Tiny lines formed across Lillian's forehead. "I can't believe someone would be so heartless to steal a baby."

Chloe got her smartphone out of her bag. "I'm going to check Facebook and see if anyone has mentioned seeing a suspicious woman in a white car. I posted a picture of me holding Emma in the hospital and put on my page that she's two months old now. I explained how she was kidnapped from here. I'll put it on Instagram too."

Henry squeezed Beth's hand and stared at Chloe. "We didn't realize you had a picture of Emma. I hope it helps to find our baby. We love Emma so much." His eyes glistened with tears as he looked directly at Chloe. "After Nora died, we were blessed when you gave us Emma to raise."

Agent Malone quickly said, "I'm sorry about your loss. What caused you to lose Nora?"

"Nora was stillborn," Beth said softly. "We don't know what caused her to die."

Chloe wondered if Henry realized she regretted giving Emma to them. It seemed he wanted to remind her that Emma was their child. She knew he loved Emma, but that didn't mean she had to forget about getting her back. In the car ride, Carter had asked her if she had signed adoption papers. She hadn't, so Beth and Henry had never officially adopted Emma. She never gave them a birth certificate, either. The birth certificate listed her and Logan as the parents.

Chloe glanced away from her cell phone and looked at Detective Benning from the Adams County offices. He was a good-looking man in his early thirties. Earlier she'd learned that he and Sheriff Lynch had been first on the scene at the schoolyard.

"Where did Sheriff Lynch disappear to? Does he have a new lead?"

"He should be back soon. He left to get a picture of the Amish woman from Noah Hershberger. Violet Robinson called and mentioned that she asked Noah to draw a picture of her. An image can be made from it so we can do a face recognition in our database to see if she has a previous criminal record." Detective Benning looked around the room. "Since she drove a car, do any of you know of a woman who was Amish but left your faith? She is probably someone who can't have children."

"Or she lost a child," Agent Malone said. "She probably appears to be a nice person and not someone you would expect could kidnap a baby. Usually the offenders are females of childbearing age with no criminal record."

Lillian put her cup of coffee on an end table. "I can't think of anyone who might have been Amish, but it seems like what the woman said to the boys about being a good mother might mean something. Karen Gibson might have disguised herself as an Amish woman and resented the boys staring at her. She was defensive because our daughter was chosen instead of her."

Chloe sighed after reading several sympathetic comments from her Facebook friends. "Nothing helpful on here or my other social networks, but as soon as we get Noah's picture, someone needs to scan it so I can put it on the Internet."

Her dad ran his fingers through his gray hair. "We should post a picture in Angie's restaurant too. Someone might recognize the woman if she's ever stopped in there."

"That's a good suggestion, Richard," her mom said, and then touched Chloe's arm. "Maybe someone saw you were pregnant and single while you worked at the restaurant. Can you think of any woman asking you questions about your pregnancy? Maybe they learned you were thinking of adoption."

"A few times customers asked me when I was due, and they weren't locals. They appeared to be tourists. No one sticks in my mind right now." Chloe didn't think the woman kidnapping Emma even realized that Beth wasn't the birth mother, but she could be wrong.

"I forgot to mention that Emma's name is embroidered on the pink blanket," Beth said. "Maybe someone will realize the woman is the kidnapper and notice the blanket too."

Chloe said, "The personalized blanket might help. I hope the woman will stop somewhere and an observant person will recognize Emma and the blanket."

"Henry's *mamm* made the blanket." Beth raised her glass of lemonade to her lips and took a big drink.

Chloe noticed her brother biting his lip. He always did that when something bothered him. "Carter, you look like you thought of something. What is it?"

Carter shrugged. "It's not important, but it just occurred to me that the woman might think if she should ever be caught that she won't go to jail. Of course, we know differently, but she might know a lot about the Amish and their beliefs. They don't believe in going to court to testify against criminals. She might think that will help her case."

"I just thought of something." Lillian's eyes widened with excitement. "Maybe the woman is really Amish but not Old Order, like we are in this district." She gave a questioning glance at Amos. "Beachy Amish drive automobiles but wear prayer coverings and Plain dresses."

Amos rolled his eyes at his wife. "You know I don't regard them as being Amish. Their beliefs are more like the Mennonite faith, but you could be right."

Agent Malone nodded. "That's interesting. I've heard of the Beachy Amish. Where is the nearest community of them? Do you know the bishop's name and his address?"

"There is a community of them about thirty miles from here." Amos stroked his gray beard. "One of our own left here a few years ago, and he ended up being the bishop."

Glancing at his smartphone, Agent Malone said, "I just received a text from the Dayton police. The Gibson couple are babysitting their niece and nephews. They seemed surprised when they were asked about Emma."

"I'm glad we know they don't have Emma." Chloe stood. "I'm going outside to watch for Tony. I got a text from him. He's on his way here."

"Wait, Miss Parrish," Detective Benning said. "I'll go outside with you. Sheriff Lynch should be getting back soon with the woman's picture."

* * *

"I really think we'll find your baby." Detective Benning adjusted the red and white cushion on the rocking chair before he sat next to Chloe. "I didn't feel comfortable saying it to you in the house."

She gave him a small smile. "I guess you could feel the tension in there too. I had to get some fresh air. I know it's my fault for wanting my baby back. I don't blame Beth and Henry for resenting me. Ever since I left Emma here with them, I've wanted to come back to get her. I thought it was better for two parents to raise her instead of a single mom. But now with what happened, I keep thinking maybe God is telling me I have a right to her."

"You definitely have a right to her. My sister's a single mom. She hadn't planned on being one. It's hard, but she's doing a great job."

"How old is your sister? I'm only eighteen."

"She's twenty-two and my nephew is four years old."

"So she got pregnant at the same age I did. I hope I get a chance to be a mom to Emma." Chloe's voice quavered. "I still can't believe my baby's been kidnapped. I hope and pray she's found soon and she'll be fine."

"It's good that the twin boys were observant. I think the woman they saw is a good lead for us."

"I hope you're right. It's been six hours already. Once the trail gets cold, it will be hard to find my baby."

"Being Amish should narrow the search, and the AMBER Alert should be a big help in finding her."

When Chloe saw Tony's car pull into the driveway, she said, "My boyfriend's here now."

"That's good he's here to give you support."

She stood and over her shoulder said, "Thank you, Detective

Benning, for talking with me."

Before Tony got to the porch, Chloe ran to him. Wearing a polo shirt and jeans, he looked so strong and handsome to her. Just having him show up to be with her during this terrible crisis made her feel better. "I'm glad you're here."

Wrapping his arms tightly around her, he said, "I got here as soon as I could. Is there any more news?"

She updated him about the possibility the woman could be a member of the Beachy Amish group, and how Beth's father mentioned there was a community of them not too far away.

"Hey, that's encouraging." Tony kissed her forehead.

"A lot of people are praying that Emma will be found and be unharmed." She dissolved into deep, racking sobs. "I wish I had never given my baby away. And now I might never see her again."

Tony pulled a white handkerchief out of his jean pocket and handed it to her.

"You always seem to be prepared. I've cried a lot on you the past couple of months."

"I take after my dad. He's always carried a handkerchief in his pocket."

She stuffed the hankie in her pocket because it was sodden with her tears. "I'll wash it before I give it back to you."

He held her tight against him and murmured, "I wish I hadn't been away when you had Emma. If my dad hadn't had a heart attack, I would've been here for you."

"Do you think it would be terrible of me to try and get Emma back? That is if my baby is found."

"You should ask Beth and Henry for your daughter. You should be the one to raise her."

Chloe lifted her head to look at Tony. "It'll break Beth's heart."

"I know, but your heart's been broken. I've hated seeing you torn up about not having Emma in your life."

"Sorry. I haven't been a very good girlfriend. And you've been the best and most understanding man ever." A thought occurred to her about Beth's pregnancy. She wondered if Tony even knew about it. Beth might not have gone yet to see a doctor, and maybe she'd taken a pregnancy test on her own. Or not. She had her own personal midwife, with Violet engaged to her brother. "Did you know Beth's pregnant?"

"No, I didn't know that."

"She's had severe morning sickness this time. I'm sure it's hard to take care of a little baby while she's not feeling well with a new pregnancy."

"That might help her realize Emma belongs with you." Tony gazed down at her, and he brushed his finger across her jaw. "I have something I need to tell you. I wanted to tell you this for months, but it never seemed like the right time before. It's not the ideal time now, but I can't wait any longer. Chloe Parrish, I love you with my whole heart. I hope there's a chance you feel the same way about me."

"I do . . . feel the same way." She'd been surprised he hadn't said these precious words to her before, because they had become so important to each other. She couldn't imagine her life without Tony in it, and if she could also have Emma, then she would never wish for anything else. Many times she'd wanted to tell him how much she loved him, but had been afraid to be the first one to say anything. But now she could freely tell him how much she loved him. "I love you too. I am thankful to God all the time that I met you. When we are apart, I hate it."

"Maybe we can change that soon, but enough talk for right now. I want to kiss the most beautiful woman I know." He lowered his mouth to hers, and gave Chloe a passionate kiss that was full of desire.

She responded without hesitation, and he deepened the kiss. A dreamy warmth rippled throughout her body. For a second, she only thought about Tony and their love for each other.

But then she remembered her baby was with a disturbed woman.

Chapter Twenty-Four

"Bridget, please hush. We'll go to Walmart soon and get other bottles. It's Mommy's fault for not buying the right ones." Jessica Thomson put the bottle on the small table by her favorite wingback chair, thinking she hated to leave her furniture at the apartment. She wanted to hit the highway late at night and go to West Virginia. *I've paid for the whole month of October. Maybe I can come back some night with a U-Haul and get the rest of my things.*

"Let's try this bottle again. You seemed to like it a little." She gently put the nipple into the baby's tiny mouth. Maybe the Amish mother breastfed her and only occasionally bottle-fed her. She noticed the woman used bottles to feed the baby at the first fundraiser, so had prepared for the baby by buying a couple different kinds of bottles and nipples.

Jessica hadn't expected to be fortunate enough to kidnap the baby today, but now that she had, it seemed she was meant to be her mommy. Happiness filled her that she had purchased Amish clothing online and made the decision to wear her disguise on this particular day. It was a stroke of genius, because the police would search for an Amish woman. It had been fairly easy to grab the baby when she noticed Beth Byler fainted, and the little girl left in charge to watch the baby went immediately to see what was wrong.

She chuckled, remembering how the adrenaline had pumped through her veins, helping her to rush to the car and leave quickly. She still couldn't believe how she'd managed to get away with no one in pursuit.

Although two Amish boys saw her, she doubted they realized she had one of their babies. Now, if she'd been dressed like she was at the first fundraiser, they might have commented that an English woman (silly how they used the word English for non-

Amish people) left with a baby around the same time as the kidnapping. And she wasn't worried about driving her car instead of a buggy. Once she saw an Amish man leave Frisch's restaurant in a car. She'd been shocked to see him driving a vehicle, so had researched it, and learned that there were communities of Plain people called Beachy Amish. It was amazing to learn that even though they wore Amish clothing, they drove automobiles and had electricity in their houses.

The authorities would never find her. She had already thrown the Plain clothing into the dumpster outside the apartment building. Then, during the time Bridget slept, she'd put as much as she could into her car for their escape.

Jessica felt relief that she'd been a good neighbor to the couple downstairs. Their annoying French poodle barked a lot, but she'd never complained to the manager. With Bridget's strong cries, the husband and wife probably wondered where the baby came from.

That stupid adoption agency didn't think I had the right temperament and background to be considered as an adopted mother for one of their clients. Well, they were wrong. I'll be the best mother ever. I won't have to be alone anymore. Bridget and I will have a great time together. She'll grow up loving me and will never realize I kidnapped her.

As soon as Bridget stopped sucking and scrunched up her face, Jessica set the bottle on the table. Maybe she needed to burp. Holding the baby against her shoulder, she patted her back. Jessica sighed when cries came out of the baby's mouth. She guessed Bridget hadn't swallowed enough milk to burp.

Although she didn't relish going to the Walmart nearby, she had to do something about her baby and buy different kinds of bottles and nipples. Obviously, the ones she had were not ones Bridget was used to. The baby needed nourishment soon.

While she murmured cooing sounds to Bridget, she cradled the child in her arms. When Jessica kissed her forehead, she noticed the baby felt warm. "Oh no, I don't have a baby thermometer to take your temperature," she said with alarm.

Quickly, she stood and walked to the kitchen counter, where she had dropped her purse earlier. She grabbed it and the pink blanket. *The night air might be cool, and I can cover Bridget with the blanket after I get her in the car seat,* she thought.

"Oh, Bridget, please don't be sick." If she should be ill, she'd buy baby Tylenol too.

Wearing her jeans and a long-sleeved blouse, she hoped no one would realize that this darling baby wasn't hers, and had once belonged to an Amish woman.

Really, if life were fair, no one would question her. Besides, that woman would probably have more children. Sure, she'd be upset about losing a baby, but soon she'd probably be popping out another infant. Before opening the apartment door, Jessica murmured, "Amish always seem to have large families, but I will only have my Bridget." She kissed the baby's cheek and said, "You'll receive more love from me than your real mother. If I hadn't been brave and taken you, you would have had a life stuck in a simple Amish home with many children all over the place. It's much better for you to be an only child and have lots of attention instead of sharing a mother's love with others."

Chapter Twenty-Five

At eight o'clock, Beth informed everyone she wasn't feeling well so would go upstairs to rest.

"I'm sorry," Chloe said, not knowing what else to say. She knew her presence made Beth uncomfortable, but she had every right to wait for word about her baby. Beth looked exhausted, and it was obvious she had an upset stomach. Earlier some of them ate sloppy joe sandwiches that Lillian had prepared, but Beth only ate a handful of pretzels. Frequently, Beth had rested her head on Henry's shoulder. It was a highly stressful situation with a mixture of law authorities, Amish, and non-Amish people all waiting anxiously for good news.

Before Beth left the living room, she glanced at Detective Benning and Agent Malone. "Please let me know immediately if there are any new developments or if they find Emma."

A few minutes after Beth and Henry left the living room, Lillian and Amos went to the phone shanty to leave messages for the rest of the family. Chloe offered her cell phone for them to use, but they said it was just as easy to use the landline phone for their calls. Chloe figured they wanted to be able to talk to their relatives in private.

As soon as the front door clicked behind them, Chloe said in a low tone of voice, "I have something I need to bring up, since Beth and her family aren't here. It might by my only chance to talk freely about a worry I have."

Tony widened his eyes. "What is it?"

Before Chloe could reply, Detective Benning's cell phone rang and he answered it. Chloe said eagerly to the others in the room, "I hope they found Emma."

After Chloe and the others watched the detective quietly nod during the conversation, he finally said, "I'll tell them. How soon will you be here?" After a pause, he said, "Sounds great. Bye, sheriff."

Detective Benning smiled broadly at Chloe. "They have Emma now and she is doing fine. The kidnapper was caught in Seaman, Ohio, and that isn't that far from here. Sheriff Lynch said they got a tip from a couple who live in an apartment below a woman named Jessica Thomson. The wife noticed Thomson carried boxes out to her car, including several baby items. The wife thought it was strange when she heard a baby cry, and wondered whose baby Thomson was watching. Then when her husband threw garbage into the apartment garbage container, he saw Amish clothing on top. Fortunately, they were aware of the AMBER Alert about Emma's kidnapping."

Chloe exhaled a deep breath. "And the sheriff is sure Emma's okay?"

Detective Benning nodded. "She appears to be. Thomson was on her way out of the apartment with the baby when they arrested her."

Chloe couldn't wait to hold Emma, and needed to express what had been on her mind the whole time she had waited for news. "Before we tell Beth and Henry, I need to say something. I want to take Emma home with us, but I promised Beth I wouldn't change my mind and want her back someday."

"That was before you had our support," her mother said, straightening her shoulders. "I want you to raise Emma and I'll help in any way I can."

Her dad said, "I will help too."

With a sad expression, her mother said, "Richard, you were right, and I should've listened to you. You believed Chloe could handle keeping Emma."

Carter moved to a vacant spot next to Chloe on the couch. He gave her a serious look. "Legally, Emma is yours. Henry and Beth have no adoption papers with your signature. Also, they never paid any of your medical expenses while you were pregnant, or any living expenses."

Agent Malone nodded. "Carter's right. When your mom mentioned to me how you had regrets about not keeping Emma, I talked to the sheriff about the issue. He plans to hand Emma over to you. Legally, she belongs to you."

"I could offer to stay for a week or two and help with everything," Chloe said. "It's obvious Beth isn't doing well taking care of a baby and being pregnant. That will give Beth and Henry time to say goodbye to Emma. I feel terrible to do this to them, but I love Emma too much to leave her here again. I could even stay at Aunt Angie's at night if Beth doesn't want me here all the time. I know it will be awkward. I hate that Emma was kidnapped, but it made me realize I need to take action now and get my baby back to be with me."

Tony took her hand in his. "I hope they agree for you to stay here so they can say goodbye, but I'm afraid they won't give her up easily. They love her as their own. I hope I'm wrong and they will be understanding."

Chloe enjoyed the feel of Tony's warm hand on hers, and squeezed his hand. "Me too. I can't stand to see anyone hurting."

"You've always had a tender heart." Her mother pushed long blonde bangs away from her face and smiled at Chloe.

"I don't want Beth to go into a deep depression like she did when she lost Nora," Chloe said.

"I'm sure it will be difficult," her mother said, "but at least Emma is only two months old. And Beth and Henry are expecting a new baby, so that should help some. I'll buy a crib, car seat, diapers, and clothes. You shouldn't take any of Emma's clothes either. They might have another little girl."

"Pam, I'd like to go with you and help you with the purchases," her dad said. "When we choose a car seat, we want to get the best with the highest safety ratings for our granddaughter."

* * *

As it happened, Beth was upstairs in the bathroom when Emma arrived in the police car.

Instantly, Chloe ran outside to get her baby. Emma was tucked in an infant car seat, and immediately Chloe unfastened the straps and gently lifted her away from the seat. Holding Emma closely to her chest, she said softly, "I've missed you so much. I love you." In spite of tears running down her face, she glanced quickly at Sheriff Lynch. "Thank you for finding and rescuing Emma from that crazy woman."

"I'm glad it turned out the way it did. Sometimes it doesn't have a happy ending," Sheriff Lynch said. "It's fortunate Thomson's neighbors realized something wasn't right and called."

Lillian smiled at the officer. "*Ya, danki.* Please come in the house to get something to eat. It's been a long day."

"I think I will. Thanks, Mrs. King."

After Lillian was out of hearing range, Sheriff Lynch said, "I didn't want to say anything in front of her, but you're welcome to use the car seat for your trip home. You can send it back with Dr. Cunningham."

"That is thoughtful of you, but as much as I'd love to take Emma home with me tonight, I think I should give Henry and Beth a few days with her. But thanks."

A few minutes later, Sheriff Lynch sat in the living room, eating a sloppy joe sandwich. In between bites, he explained, "Jessica Thomson wanted a baby and assumed she could get away with it if she snatched an Amish baby. She's English but knew that Beachy Amish drive cars."

With Emma in her arms, Chloe sat on one of the upholstered chairs. As she listened to the officer, she still couldn't believe that Jessica Thomson had grabbed her baby. How could she steal another woman's child? She must have been one desperate woman to commit this crime.

"Did she put up any resistance?" Agent Malone asked.

Sheriff Lynch shook his head. "She didn't put up any fuss. The Seaman police told me that she was still in the apartment parking lot when they got there. At that time, Thomson planned to get different bottles for Emma. Apparently, the baby didn't like the bottles she had. Thomson thought Emma might be running a fever, so she planned on getting a thermometer too. By the way, Thomson referred to Emma as Bridget."

Lillian stood and said, "Chloe, I'll get a bottle ready for you to feed her. I'm surprised she's not crying. It sounds like she didn't get fed enough."

"Emma doesn't act sick," Chloe's mother said. "I hope she doesn't have a temperature."

Sheriff Lynch said, "She doesn't have a fever. A doctor on staff at the hospital examined her and said she was fine. She sure is a cute baby."

"She looks like you did at that age, Chloe," her dad said, smiling at her. "You were a pretty baby and good-natured too."

As soon as Beth entered the living room, she frowned at Chloe. "I was only gone for a few minutes to use the bathroom. I can't believe I missed my moment to welcome Emma home and to hold her."

"The important thing is she's here now," Carter said. "Our prayers were answered."

Chloe ignored Beth's jealous comment, but wished she could tell her that she had every right to hold her daughter. *It is my fault for making such a difficult situation. I never should have given Emma to Beth.* Relief went through Chloe's heart that she could finally hold her baby. As she cuddled Emma and kissed her little face several times, she silently gave thanks to God for her baby's safe return. Tears filled her eyes again as she gazed at Emma, then she glanced around at her family. "I'm so happy."

"Here's the bottle," Lillian said as she entered the room.

Beth held out her hand to take the bottle from her mother. "I can feed Emma."

"Thanks, but I'll feed her," Chloe said quickly.

Lillian handed her the bottle, and Chloe noticed that Beth's face was flushed. Even though it was obvious that Beth wasn't happy about not being the one to hold and feed Emma, Chloe definitely couldn't relinquish her baby.

Lillian said to Beth, "Your dad and I are going to leave. We can all sleep well tonight and be thankful Emma's here. It's a blessing that she was found already."

"Where is *Daed*?" Beth asked.

"As soon as he saw Emma was fine, he went to hitch Thunder to our buggy. Henry went with him. It's been a long day and tomorrow is church day." Lillian gave Beth a hug. "I hope you'll feel well enough to attend."

"I'll be happy to watch Emma while you and Henry go to church," Chloe said. *I want Beth to realize I need to be with my daughter.*

"That's a *gut* idea," Lillian said.

In a sharp voice, Beth said, "We can take Emma with us to church."

"I'm planning on staying several days. I can sleep at my aunt's house, but I'll be around to take care of Emma and to help with anything you need done. I can even stay here some nights so you don't have to get up in the middle of the night to feed Emma." Chloe watched Beth's face to see her reaction, and observed she turned an even darker red.

"You don't need to stick around. I'm capable of taking care of my baby. She won't be kidnapped again."

Chloe's mother said, "Beth, maybe it's better to be upfront with you now. Today has been so stressful for everyone that I know Chloe wanted to wait before bringing something up to you and Henry. I've heard Chloe cry for the last two months for her baby. She wanted to keep her, but I encouraged her to choose adoption. She has regretted not keeping Emma. It's my fault for not giving the support she needed, but we now see how important it is to Chloe to have her daughter with her. She can give you a week to spend with Emma to say goodbye before she takes her home, and will help you take care of her during this time."

Henry walked into the room with anger flickering in his eyes. "I can't believe what I just heard. Chloe, you gave us Emma. You can't expect us to give her back to you. When you didn't want her, we accepted her as our own child. We love her."

Chloe glanced away from Emma to stare at Henry. "But you're wrong. I always wanted my baby, but at the time of her birth I didn't have the support I needed."

"Because Chloe never signed any adoption papers, she is still legally Emma's mother," Carter said in a patient and kind voice. "I think this can be discussed more tomorrow, and the best way to handle the situation can be all sorted out. My parents and I are staying at my aunt's, and we won't leave until tomorrow afternoon."

Chloe noticed Emma stopped sucking, so she removed the bottle from her mouth. Emma gave her an adorable smile. "She's smiling at me." Chloe felt her heart would burst with happiness at seeing her baby smile.

Beth whispered to Henry, "Why is Emma smiling now?"

As Chloe smiled back at Emma, she wondered what Beth meant. Did she wonder why the baby would smile at a mother she hadn't seen since birth? Maybe Emma recognized her voice. While pregnant with Emma, she'd talked to her frequently in soothing voices and sung her lullabies.

* * *

Beth and Henry followed her mom out to the buggy. "*Mamm*, Emma smiled at Chloe . . . a beautiful smile. She has smiled in her sleep and when she has passed gas, but not a smile like she gave Chloe. It was a genuine smile. I've been waiting for her to give me a real smile."

"I'm sure Emma will smile at you that way," Henry said. "It's because she was hungry and finally got milk after hours of being away from her home."

Her mom stopped by the buggy. "That makes sense, what Henry said."

Beth shrugged, not convinced that was the reason for Emma smiling at Chloe, but she needed to talk to her parents before they left. She leaned against the buggy's door and saw her *daed* was anxious to leave. "*Daed*, I need to talk to you and *Mamm* before you go home. When you were outside, we learned that Chloe wants to stay here for a week to help with Emma and give us time to say goodbye. After that, Chloe plans on taking Emma home with them. Her lawyer brother even told us how legally Emma belongs to Chloe because she never signed any adoption papers. What can we do? I don't want Chloe to take Emma away from us. I love her so much. Doesn't a verbal agreement count for something?"

The moon cast a soft light on the buggy, and Beth saw how troubled her *daed* looked at the news about Chloe wanting her baby.

"I'm sorry, Beth. It doesn't seem fair when you took the baby to raise as your own. If you want me to talk to Chloe on yours and Henry's behalf, I will. I'll tell them what a good mother you have been and how much love you have both given her." He hesitated, then continued, "But my heart won't be in it, because it seems once that woman kidnapped Emma, things changed. Chloe and her family realized how important family is in a time of crisis. When Emma was missing, they came together. It wasn't Chloe coming here by herself."

Beth spoke in a choked voice, "But I can't lose another baby."

Gently, her father said, "I understand. It's a big blow, but I wouldn't be surprised if Dr. Cunningham and Chloe get married. If that happens it won't be the same, but we will get to see Emma."

Her mom hugged her again and climbed into the buggy. "I'm afraid I agree. And you need to take care of the new life inside you. You don't want to faint again, and you need to get a full night's sleep. I'm glad you are getting an ultrasound. I want to be with you when it's done."

Fingering the brim of his hat, her *daed* said, "Remember your faith and give your burdens up to God. Pray for Him to mend your heart. He will see you through this ordeal. When I'm troubled, I repeat the first verse from Psalms 46: 'God is my refuge and strength, an ever-present help in trouble.' I love you and God loves you."

Beth saw a look of tenderness cross her *daed's* face. "I love you too."

"We had better go. I might be preaching tomorrow." Her *daed* held the reins with one hand and clucked to Thunder.

Beth watched for a moment as the buggy moved down their driveway. When she could no longer see the back buggy taillights, Beth said, "I'm not going to church tomorrow. I want to spend what little time I have left with Emma." In a resigned voice, Beth said, "I'll tell Chloe she can come in the afternoon."

Epilogue

Three Months Later

Chloe sat on the leather chair folding Emma's clean clothes that she'd just taken out of the dryer. She placed separate piles of bibs, onesies, and other baby items on the coffee table while her mother sat across from her holding Emma. Chloe watched her mother reciting the nursery rhyme pat-a-cake to Emma. It was fun hearing her daughter laugh each time her mom touched Emma's belly and said, "Bake it in the oven for Emma and me."

A whiff of Italian cooking made her realize how hungry she was. In the kitchen, her dad was putting finishing touches on the food for the celebration dinner. After Tony's proposal to her only a week ago, on New Year's Eve, her parents had invited Ray and Evelyn Cunningham to their house for this Saturday evening. When Tony's parents had come to see her and Emma during the holidays, Chloe felt sure that Tony was going to pop the question sometime around Christmas. Of course, she also had thought he might ask her to marry him on her nineteenth birthday in November, but waiting until New Year's Eve had been a fantastic idea of his.

She would remember forever the wonderful moment when Tony's proposal had happened in a fancy restaurant in Cincinnati. Candles and fragrant flowers rested on their table. She wore a classy red dress and he looked handsome in a suit. When his face became serious, she just knew what would happen next. Thankfully, she wasn't disappointed when Tony said, "Chloe Parrish, I love you more than anything, and I will for the rest of my life. And you know I love Emma too. With the beginning of the New Year, I want this to be a special night for us. Will you marry me?"

"Yes, I'll marry you. I love you, Tony. I can't imagine a life without you."

He popped open a ring box, and inside was a princess-cut diamond ring. Under the candlelight, it sparkled. Soon after his proposal, Tony asked if he could adopt Emma and become her father legally. After Emma was with her for a month, she told Logan to come see their baby during his college break. He'd never visited Chloe to see his daughter, so she was confident Logan wouldn't protest Tony adopting Emma.

Since it had only been a week since he gave her the engagement ring, they hadn't decided on a date. Chloe and Tony discussed a summer wedding, because they were anxious to become a family and not have to commute any longer to see each other. Chloe's mother suggested a longer engagement might be better for both of them. Her mother wanted her to start going to college part-time. She'd explained it wouldn't do for Chloe not to have a college education when she was marrying a doctor. Instead of getting angry that her mother had mentioned college again, she'd smiled and said, "It's okay, Mom. I'll take college courses sometime, and might even graduate with a degree. I've been thinking about becoming a high school science teacher."

Glancing again at her mom and Emma, Chloe realized as much as she wanted to get married, it was nice spending time with her parents and siblings. Andrea and Carter popped in on a regular basis to see Emma. From her chair in the living room, Chloe got a glimpse of her dad eating a spoonful of sauce. "Dad, don't eat the sauce. I want enough for our spaghetti."

He grinned. "I have to sample it to make sure my famous sauce tastes as good as always."

Her mom stopped clapping Emma's hands for a moment. "Your sauce is always good, Richard."

When her dad had made several visits a week to see her and Emma, Chloe knew it wasn't just them he wanted to be with, but her mom too. Emma gave her grandparents an excuse to spend time together. Finally, on one snowy evening in November, Chloe's mom said, "Richard, you don't need to drive in this weather to go to Carter's. Just stay here. Really, there's no point in

you looking for a house. You should move back here. Chloe and
Emma would love for you to move back home." At his huge grin,
her mom said, "Okay, I want you to live here too."

Chloe was happy that Emma had something to do with their
reconciliation. After pushing for adoption before, her parents
couldn't seem to see Emma enough now. Even though her mother
was the CEO at the cancer clinic, she gave more responsibilities to
Andrea and the other doctors. After the kidnapping, her mother
wanted to have more time for family.

Tony entered the room and stood next to Chloe's chair. "I
finished making my phone calls. No medical emergencies."

"I'm glad."

"My parents called and are only a few miles away."

"They might get here before my siblings arrive."

He leaned down and gave her a kiss, then whispered in her ear,
"Let's elope next month."

"As tempting as that is, we can't elope. I'm breastfeeding
Emma." It hadn't been easy at first, but Emma had finally learned
to nurse. Although Chloe knew breastfeeding wouldn't make up
for the two-month separation she had caused, she became
determined to have milk for Emma.

"We could take Emma with us, but I suppose we should wait."
He gave her an irresistible, boyish grin. "You look gorgeous in
that dress."

When going through her closet, she'd decided to wear a dress
for their engagement celebration with family. She grinned at Tony.
"You bought it for me, but I'm glad you like me in it."

"I'll see if I can steal Emma from your mom. She's such a
baby hog," Tony said.

Chloe's mom said, "I heard that."

When Tony took Emma in his arms, she smiled at him. Tears
filled Chloe's eyes as she realized how blessed she was to have
Emma back and to have Tony in her life. At the beginning of last
summer, she'd been depressed about her pregnancy and living in a
small town. Fields Corner was not her idea of a fun time when
she should have been in Europe.

It was amazing how God had turned her despair into joy. He

loved her and gave her Emma and Tony. And when they married, she knew God would bless their union as husband and wife.

* * *

Beth and Henry sat on chairs next to an oak table in the corner of their living room. Since it was just the two of them, Beth wasn't wearing her *kapp*, and her brown hair hung down her back. She loved this time in the early evening when they played a board game or worked on a puzzle. Then they usually spent time reading Scripture and saying prayers together before going upstairs to bed.

After Beth put a piece in the jigsaw puzzle, she smiled at Henry. "I'm glad Chloe gave us this Thomas Kinkade puzzle for a Christmas present."

"It was nice of her."

"And it was *wunderbaar* she brought Emma when she gave us our Christmas gifts. Chloe's been great about visiting us when she comes to Field Corners to see Tony."

"I'm glad we still get to see Emma." Henry pushed down a piece next to Beth's. "We've made a lot of progress on this puzzle."

"*Ya*, we've made a lot of progress . . . in other ways too. I never thought we could forgive Chloe, but we both did." Beth touched her baby bump. "Learning that I was carrying twins helped. I realized then having a newborn plus being pregnant with two babies might be too much for me some days. When we saw them on the screen, it was incredible. I was speechless."

"Your jaw dropped when the technician pointed to the two images."

"It was nice you took me out to lunch after the ultrasound."

Henry laughed. "I realized you were in shock because I thought you would refuse to go to lunch. I knew you had been anxious to get home to be with Emma."

On the day she'd had the ultrasound, Chloe offered to stay with Emma. Without her car or an infant car seat, Beth trusted Chloe wouldn't leave and would keep her promise to give them several days to say goodbye to Emma. She couldn't imagine Chloe being so low as to hurry get a ride to Cincinnati for her and Emma while they were away. "I decided I better eat a good lunch with having two babies needing nutrition while my stomach wasn't queasy. Besides, it was fun having lunch with you."

"You shocked me when you bought a piece of chocolate pie to take home to Chloe."

Beth shrugged. "Chloe was surprised too. She eyed it as if she thought I'd poisoned it. I remembered how much she loved the chocolate pie the first time we ate at the bakery.

"This new year will be a *wunderbaar* one for us with two babies. I never expected God would give us two *kinner* so soon after losing Nora Marie and Emma."

Picking up another piece to fit into the lighthouse image, she looked again at Henry. "I should have realized Chloe wouldn't be able to live without Emma. All the time she was considering adoption, she constantly said how much she wanted to keep her baby."

"We didn't have much time to discuss it. Chloe went into labor soon after she asked us to raise her daughter."

Beth let her thoughts slip back to the day Chloe took Emma. It was four days after the kidnapping when Chloe's mom had returned to Fields Corner. Beth's bottom lip quivered and tears escaped down her cheeks while Mrs. Parrish had fastened Emma in the infant seat. Beth remembered how Chloe had hugged her and said, *I'm sorry for the pain I've caused you and Henry. Please someday forgive me.*

Looking up from the puzzle, Beth stared at Henry. "Even though we didn't get to keep Emma, I'm glad we had her for the time we did. Do you think if Emma hadn't been kidnapped, Chloe never would have taken her from us?"

Henry shook his head. "I think it was going to happen sometime anyhow. When she and Tony fell *in lieb*, Chloe then realized she could give Emma a life with two parents."

"I have to hand it to her that she's breastfeeding Emma. I never thought of attempting to pump for weeks like she did, so I could feed Emma my milk."

Henry picked up another piece and placed it in the puzzle. "It was nice for me to give Emma a bottle when you were busy."

"*Ya*, I loved seeing you hold Emma." She giggled. "With your big hands, you should be able to hold our two babies at the same time."

He grinned. "I'm also able to lift my very pregnant *fraa* into the buggy."

Glancing down at her belly, she said, "I'm definitely huge already. I'm glad my nausea subsided so I can enjoy eating."

Henry reached across the table and took her hands in his. "I love you, Beth. I'm so thankful that I married you, and that we are expecting twins."

Beth smiled with satisfaction that God had blessed her with Henry and her babies . . . the two she had lost and the unborn ones she already loved. Although the path to this point had been rocky, God had never left her. Squeezing Henry's hands, she said, "I love you too."

Dear Reader,

Thank you for reading my novel, *Amish Baby Snatched*. Special blessings have resulted from the friendships that I have with my readers. I appreciate more than you will ever know—the nice comments on Facebook, email messages, and cards. I give thanks to God for my readers and for giving me the words to write in my books.

While writing *Amish Baby Snatched*, I loved sharing how two young women from different worlds could become close friends. There were moments when I could not keep the tears from falling. I felt deeply Chloe's pain at not getting the support she wanted from her parents and boyfriend Logan. Even when she felt unloved at times, she always knew God loved her unconditionally.

Writing about Beth's sadness at having a stillborn was another time I cried. Losing a child at any time is heart wrenching, and for Beth to lose her firstborn is particularly difficult.

It doesn't matter where we find ourselves on our journey in this life and what challenges fall in our path; we are never alone. God is with us if we allow Him in our hearts.

Blessings,
Diane

Delicious Amish Cinnamon Bread

Ingredients

1 cup butter, softened
2 cups sugar
2 eggs
2 cups buttermilk or 2 cups milk plus 2 tablespoons vinegar or lemon juice
4 cups flour
2 teaspoons baking soda

Cinnamon/sugar mixture:

2/3 cups sugar
2 teaspoons cinnamon

Directions

Preheat oven to 350 degrees.
Cream together butter, 2 cups of sugar and 2 eggs. Add milk, flour and baking soda. Blend until completely combined.
Put 1/2 of the batter into two greased loaf pans. (Basically pour 1/4 of the total batter into each pan.)
Mix in a small bowl the 2/3 cup of sugar and cinnamon. Sprinkle 3/4 of cinnamon mixture on the top of the batter in each pan.
Pour (or scoop!) remaining batter to pans. Sprinkle with the remaining cinnamon mixture. Swirl with knife.
Bake for 45-50 minutes or until toothpick comes out clean.
Cool in pans for 20 minutes before removing from pans.

My daughter-in-law, Lea, made this bread for us after my husband's hip surgery. We couldn't stop eating this moist and yummy bread.

Other Books by Diane Craver

Amish Fiction
Dreams of Plain Daughters series
A Joyful Break, Book One
Judith's Place, Book Two
Fleeting Hope, Book Three
A Decision of Faith, Book Four

An Amish Starry Christmas Night
An Amish Starry Summer Night

Christian Romance
Marrying Mallory
When Love Happens Again

Chick-Lit Mystery
A Fiery Secret

Contemporary Romance
Whitney in Charge
Never the Same
The Proposal
Yours or Mine

Historical and Christian Fiction
A Gift Forever
Visit Diane online!

Websites:
http://www.dianecraver.com
http://www.dianecraver.com/blog
Facebook:
https://www.facebook.com/#!/pages/Diane-
Craver/153906208887

CPSIA information can be obtained
at www.ICGtesting.com
Printed in the USA
BVHW072242261118
534073BV00001B/211

9 781530 387052